OuR
ToWN

Thornton Wilder

OuR ToWN

A Play in Three Acts

HARPER**PERENNIAL** MODERN**CLASSICS**

NEW YORK • LONDON • TORONTO • SYDNEY • NEW DELHI • AUCKLAND

A hardcover edition of *Our Town* was first published by Coward-McCann, Inc., in 1938.

A revised hardcover edition was published by Harper & Brothers in 1957. It is reprinted here by arrangement with the Wilder Family LLC.

OUR TOWN. Copyright © 1938, 1965 by the Wilder Family LLC. Foreword copyright © 2003, 2013 by Donald Margulies. Afterword copyright © 2003, 2013 by Tappan Wilder. A Nephew's Note © 2020 by Tappan Wilder. All rights reserved. Printed in the United States of America. No part of this book may be used or reproduced in any manner whatsoever without written permission except in the case of brief quotations embodied in critical articles and reviews. For information address HarperCollins Publishers Inc., 195 Broadway, New York, NY 10007. HarperCollins books may be purchased for educational, business, or sales promotional use. For information please e-mail the Special Markets Department at SPsales@harpercollins.com.

FIRST PERENNIAL LIBRARY EDITION PUBLISHED 1985.
FIRST PERENNIAL CLASSICS EDITION PUBLISHED 1998; REISSUED 2003.
FIRST HARPER PERENNIAL MODERN CLASSICS EDITION PUBLISHED 2013, REISSUED 2020.

The Library of Congress has catalogued a previous edition of this book as follows:

Wilder, Thornton.
    Our town : a play in three acts / Thornton Wilder.—Current Perennial Classics ed.
        p. cm.—(Perennial classics)
    ISBN 0-06-051263-6
    1. New Hampshire—Drama. 2. City and town life—Drama.
    3. Young women—Drama. I. Title. II. Perennial classic.
    PS3545.I34509   2003
    812'.52—dc22 2003055676

ISBN 978-0-06-300399-6 (pbk.)

22 23 24 25 26 LBC 14 13 12 11 10

To Alexander Woolcott
of Castleton Township, Rutland County, Vermont

Contents

—◦◦◦—

Foreword

You are holding in your hands a great American play. Possibly, *the* great American play.

If you think you're already familiar with *Our Town*, chances are you read it long ago, in sixth or seventh grade, when it was lumped in a tasting portion of slim, palatable volumes of American literature along with *The Red Pony* by John Steinbeck and Edith Wharton's *Ethan Frome*. You were compelled to read it, like nasty medicine force-fed for your own good, when you were too young to appreciate how enriching it might be. Or perhaps you saw one too many amateur productions that, to put it kindly, failed to persuade you of the play's greatness. You sneered at the domestic activities of the citizenry of Grover's Corners, New Hampshire, and rolled your eyes at the quaint-seeming romance between George Gibbs and Emily Webb. You dismissed *Our Town* as a corny relic of Americana and relegated Thornton Wilder to the kitsch bin along with Norman Rockwell and Frank Capra.

You may have come around on Capra (*It's a Wonderful Life* actually owes a great deal to *Our Town*), and you may now be able to credit Rockwell for being a fine illustrator even if you can't quite bring yourself to call him an artist, but Wilder is another story. In your mind he remains the eternal schoolmaster preaching old-fashioned values to a modern public that knows far more than he does, and you remain steadfast in your skepticism of his importance to American literature.

You are not alone.

I have a confession to make: I didn't always appreciate the achievement of Thornton Wilder, either. Like many of you, I had read *Our Town* when I was too young and had seen it a few times. I thought I knew it and, frankly, didn't think much of it; I didn't get what was so great about it. That is, until I happened to see the 1988 Lincoln Center Theater production, directed by Gregory Mosher, an experience which remains one of the most memorable of my theatergoing life. I was so mesmerized by its subversive power, so warmed by its wisdom, so shattered by its third act, that I couldn't believe it was the same play I thought I had known since childhood. I went home and reread the masterpiece that had been on my shelf all along, and pored over the text to see what Mosher and his troupe of actors (led by Spalding Gray as the Stage Manager) had done differently. As far as I could tell, they had changed very little. *I* was the one who had changed. By the late eighties, I had entered my thirties and had a foothold in life; I had buried both my parents; I had protested a devastating war; and I had fallen in love. In other words, I had lived enough of a life to finally understand what was so great about *Our Town*.

"The response we make when we 'believe' a work of the imagination," Wilder wrote, "is that of saying: 'This is the way things are. I have always known it without being fully aware that I knew it. Now in the presence of this play or novel or poem (or picture or piece of music) I know that I know it.' "

Wilder was right: *I believed every word of it.*

—⚬—

One of the many joys of teaching is that you get to introduce students to work you admire. Since you can never relive the experience of seeing or hearing or reading a work of art for the first time, you can do the next best thing: you can teach it. And, through the discoveries your students make, you can recapture, vicariously, some of the exhilaration that accompanied your own discovery of that work long ago.

I teach playwriting to undergraduates at Yale. In addition to weekly writing assignments and a term project, my students read, and together we dissect, a variety of contemporary American and English plays (all personal favorites)—Harold Pinter's *Betrayal;* David Mamet's *Glengarry Glen Ross;* John Guare's *Six Degrees of Separation;* three plays by Caryl Churchill: *Fen, Top Girls,* and *Mad Forest;* Tennessee Williams's *Cat on a Hot Tin Roof;* Wallace Shawn's *Aunt Dan and Lemon;* Chris Durang's *Marriage of Bette and Boo;* and Anna Deavere Smith's *Fires in the Mirror* among them—each of which provides rich areas for discussion about structure, character, event, theme, story, style.

A few years ago I added *Our Town* to the list. I schedule it at the end by devious design: after our semester-long exploration of What Makes a Good Play, I sneak in a truly great one. Only I don't *tell* them it's a great one. "Why did you assign this play?" they demand to know. "Nothing happens." "It's dated." "Simplistic." "Sentimental."

I have them where I want them. Now I can give myself the pleasure of persuading them that they've got it all wrong, that the opposite of their criticisms is true: *Our Town* is anything but dated, it is timeless; it *is* simple, but also profound; it is full of genuine sentiment, which is not the same as its being sentimental; and, as far as its being uneventful, well, the event of the play is huge: it's life itself.

Like many works of great art, its greatness can be deceptive: a bare stage, spare language, archetypal characters. "Our
claim, our hope, our despair are in the mind," Wilder wrote,
"not in 'scenery.' " Indeed, he begins the play with: "No curtain. No scenery." It is important to recognize the thunder-
clap those words amounted to. Consider the context: The
play was written in 1937, when stage directions like that were
still largely unheard of in American dramaturgy. The season
Our Town graced Broadway, the other notable plays were
now-forgotten boulevard comedies by Philip Barry and Clare
Boothe (*Here Come the Clowns* and *Kiss the Boys Goodbye*,
respectively), and melodramas by now-forgotten playwrights
E. P. Conkle and Paul Vincent Carroll (*Prologue to Glory*
and *Shadow and Substance*). Wilder alone was challenging
the potential of theater. An old-fashioned writer? Thornton
Wilder was radical! A visionary!

In his 1957 introduction to *Three Plays,* Wilder wrote
of the loss of theatergoing pleasure he began to experience
in the decade before writing *Our Town,* when he "ceased to
believe in the stories [he] saw presented there. . . . The theatre was not only inadequate, it was evasive. . . . I found the
word for it: it aimed to be *soothing.* The tragic had no heat;
the comic had no bite; the social criticism failed to indict us
with responsibility." (Has our theater really changed all that
much since Wilder wrote those words? The same claim could
be made today, given the "soothing" fare that dominates a
Broadway where the "serious" play is the anomaly.)

Stripping the stage of fancy artifice, Wilder set himself
a formidable challenge. With two ladders, a few pieces of
furniture, and a minimum of props, he attempted "to find a
value above all price for the smallest events in our daily life."
Actors mimed their stage business; a "stage manager" func-
tioned as both omniscient narrator and player. These ideas

were startlingly modern for American drama in 1937. True, Pirandello broke down the conventions of the play fifteen years earlier, in Europe, in *Six Characters in Search of an Author* (the world premiere of which Wilder attended), and in the United States in the decade before *Our Town,* O'Neill tested the bounds of theatrical storytelling, with mixed results, in *Strange Interlude.* But with *Our Town,* Wilder exploded the accepted notions of character and story, and catapulted the American drama into the twentieth century. He did for the stage what Picasso and Braque's experiments in cubism did for painting and Joyce's stream of consciousness did for the novel. To mistake him for a traditionalist is to do Thornton Wilder an injustice. He was, in fact, a modernist who translated European and Asian ideas about theater into the American idiom.

By 1930, Wilder, who started his writing career as a novelist, had begun experimenting with dramatic form. Influenced by the economy of storytelling of Noh drama, he boldly compressed ninety years of a family's history into twenty minutes of stage time in *The Long Christmas Dinner.* His 1931 one-act, *Pullman Car Hiawatha,* which brings to life with a minimum of scenery a section of a train car and some of its passengers, reads as a marvelous rehearsal for many of the ideas he put to confident use in *Our Town;* it is also a fascinating play in its own right. In it, Wilder is in remarkably fertile fettle: chairs serve as berths in the Pullman car; actors represent the planets and passing fields and towns (including a Grover's Corners, Ohio); a stage manager is present (there's one in *The Happy Journey to Trenton and Camden,* too); a ghost makes an appearance, that of a German immigrant worker who perished while helping to build a trestle the train crosses; and, perhaps most strikingly, a young woman—a prototype for Emily—dies unexpectedly on the journey. The woman cries to the archangels Gabriel and Michael, who have arrived to escort her to her final destination, "I haven't done anything with my life . . . I haven't realized anything," before accepting her fate. "I see now," she says finally. "I see now. I understand everything now."

Anyone who dismisses *Our Town* as an idealized view of American life has failed to see the impieties and hypocrisies depicted in Wilder's vision. "Oh, Mama, you never tell us the truth about anything," Emily bemoans to her mother.

Simon Stimson, the alcoholic choirmaster, is a brilliant creation, buffoon and tragic figure all at once. He is not a stumbling town drunk designed for easy laughs; rather, he is a tortured, self-destructive soul whose cries for help are ignored by a provincial people steeped in denial. In the tragedy of Simon Stimson—a suicide, we learn in Act III— Wilder illustrates the failure of society to help its own and the insidiousness of systematic ignorance. "The only thing the rest of us can do," Mrs. Gibbs opines about Stimson's public drunkenness, "is just not to notice it." We may laugh at her Yankee pragmatism but it is also chilling.

The perfection of the play starts with its title. Grover's Corners belongs to all of us; it is indeed *our* town, a microcosm of the human family, genus American. But in that specificity it becomes all towns. Everywhere. Indeed, the play's success across cultural borders around the world attests to its being something much greater than an American play: it is a play that captures the universal experience of being alive.

The Stage Manager tells us the play's action begins on May 7, 1901, but it is as specific to that time as it was, no doubt, to 1937, and as it is to the time in which we're living. The three-act structure is a marvel of economy: Act I is dubbed "Daily Life," Act II, "Love and Marriage," and Act III, "I reckon you can guess what that's about."

The simultaneity of life and death, past, present, and future pervades *Our Town*. As soon as we are introduced to Doc and Mrs. Gibbs, the Stage Manager informs us of their deaths. Minutes into the play and already the long shadow of death is cast, ironizing all that follows. With the specter of mortality hovering, the quotidian business of the people of Grover's Corners attains a kind of grandeur.

When eleven-year-old Joe Crowell, the newsboy, enters, making his rounds, he and Doc Gibbs chat about the weather, the boy's teacher's impending marriage, and the condition of his pesky knee. The prosaic turns suddenly wrenching when the Stage Manager casually fills us in on young Joe's future, his scholarship to MIT, his graduating at the top of his class. "Goin' to be a great engineer, Joe was. But the war broke out and he died in France.—All that education for nothing." How could anyone accuse Wilder of sentimentality when he, like life, is capable of such cruelty? In just a few eloquent sentences he captures both the capriciousness of life and the futility of war. The war Wilder referred to, of course, was the Great War—the world was between wars when he wrote *Our Town*—but the poignancy of the newsboy's fate is felt perhaps even more exquisitely today, in light of all the death and destruction the world has endured since.

Note the audacious and surprising ways in which Wilder has structured his acts; he interrupts the narrative flow of each with a stylistic departure. In Act I, Professor Willard and Editor Webb offer discursive sidebars about the geography and sociology of Grover's Corners, a device reminiscent of the collagist technique of newsreel and newspaper snippets employed by his contemporary, the novelist John Dos Passos, in his *U.S.A.* trilogy.

At the start of the second act, it is three years later, George and Emily's wedding day. The Stage Manager interrupts the frantic preparations to show us "how all this began. . . . I'm awfully interested in how big things like that begin." And he takes us back in time to the drugstore-counter conversation the couple had "when they first knew that . . . they were meant for one another." Once that seminal event is re-created, we return to the wedding itself. Emily, the bride with cold feet, plaintively asks her father, "Why can't I stay for a while just as I am," expressing the ageless, heartbreaking, child's wish to prolong the charmed state of childhood and stave off the harshness of the adult world.

The passage from Love and Marriage to Death is as abrupt and wrenching as it is in real life. The people whose vitality moved and amused us before intermission are now coolly seated in rows in the town cemetery. Mrs. Gibbs, Simon Stimson, and Mrs. Soames, "who enjoyed the wedding so," are all dead now, as is Wally Webb, whose young life was cut short by a burst appendix while on a Boy Scout camping trip.

Much as the soda-fountain flashback is the centerpiece of the second act, Emily's posthumous visit to the past in the middle of Act III provides the emotional climax of the play. Newly deceased while giving birth to her second child, Emily wishes to go back to a happy day and chooses her twelfth birthday. The dead warn her that such a return can only be painful. The job of the dead, they tell her, is to forget the living. Emily learns all too quickly that they are right and decides to join the indifferent dead. Her farewell is one of the immortal moments in all of American drama:

Good-by, Good-by, world. Good-by, Grover's Corners . . . Mama and Papa. Good-by to clocks ticking . . . and Mama's sunflowers. And food and coffee. And new-ironed dresses and hot baths . . .

and sleeping and waking up. Oh, earth, you're too wonderful for anybody to realize you.

Wilder modestly wrote, "I am not one of the new dramatists we are looking for. I wish I were. I hope I have played a part in preparing the way for them." He was wrong about not being one of the "new dramatists." In some respects he was the *first* American playwright. The part he played in preparing those who followed—Williams, Miller, Albee, Wilson (Lanford), Wilson (August), Vogel, to list a few—is incalculable.

"The cottage, the go-cart, the Sunday-afternoon drives in the Ford, the first rheumatism, the grandchildren, the second rheumatism, the deathbed, the reading of the will,"—it's all here, all in *Our Town,* all the passages of life.

If you are new to *Our Town,* I envy you. A joyous discovery awaits you.

Welcome—or welcome back—to *Our Town.*

—Donald Margulies
New Haven, Connecticut

Addendum to the Foreword of the 75th Anniversary Edition

—〰—

A little more than ten years ago, when I first approached the daunting task of writing a foreword to *Our Town*, the aftershocks of 9/11 were still being felt; my reading of the play at that time was very much colored by that calamitous event. Thornton Wilder's 1938 meditation on life, love and marriage, and death in a small New Hampshire town in the early part of the twentieth century seemed to illuminate uncannily the experience of being alive in the twenty-first. (Indeed, there was a resurgence of interest in the play and a spate of productions worldwide, including David Cromer's revelatory mounting in 2009.)

Today, as I contemplate the play anew for this addendum, a different horror casts its shadow over the pages of *Our Town*: the massacre of twenty children and six adults at the Sandy Hook Elementary School in Newtown, Connecticut. When that terrible incident occurred, just a few weeks prior to this writing, I couldn't help but think of *Our Town*. Maybe it was the New England setting with the universal-sounding Newtown standing in for Grover's Corners. I imagined a typical, tranquil town, peopled with decent citizens, suddenly seeing their world shattered and their beloved children brutally, inexplicably, taken away from them. The simple truths about family and community Wilder wrote about seventy-five years ago seemed to articulate the enormity of this contemporary tragedy.

Our Town celebrates life in all its mundane profundity. Something as seemingly inconsequential as Mrs. Gibbs's exasperated call to her children to come down to breakfast can produce tears of identification. A Boy Scout camping trip is tragically cut short. A trip to Paris is never taken. Childbirth ends in death.

"Do any human beings ever realize life while they live it?—every, every minute?" Emily asks through her tears. "No," the Stage Manager curtly replies. "The saints and poets, maybe—they do some."

—Donald Margulies
New Haven, Connecticut
January 3, 2013

Donald Margulies won the 2000 Pulitzer Prize for Drama for *Dinner with Friends* and was a finalist twice before with *Sight Unseen* and *Collected Stories*. His other plays include *The Country House, Coney Island Christmas, Time Stands Still, Shipwrecked! An Entertainment, Brooklyn Boy,* and *The Loman Family Picnic*. Mr. Margulies is an adjunct professor of English and Theatre Studies at Yale University.

The first performance of this play took place at the McCarter Theatre, Princeton, New Jersey, on January 22, 1938. The first New York performance was at Henry Miller's Theatre, February 4, 1938. It was produced and directed by Jed Harris. The technical drirector was Raymond Sovey; the costumes were designed by Madame Hélène Pons. The role of the Stage Manager was played by Frank Craven. The Gibbs family were played by Jay Fassett, Evelyn Varden, John Craven and Marilyn Erskine; the Webb family by Thomas Ross, Helen Carew, Martha Scott (as Emily), and Charles Wiley, Jr.; Mrs. Soames was played by Doro Merande; Simon Stimson by Philip Coolidge.

CHARACTERS (in the order of their appearance)

STAGE MANAGER
DR. GIBBS
JOE CROWELL
HOWIE NEWSOME
MRS. GIBBS
MRS. WEBB
GEORGE GIBBS
REBECCA GIBBS
WALLY WEBB
EMILY WEBB
PROFESSOR WILLARD
MR. WEBB
WOMAN IN THE BALCONY
MAN IN THE AUDITORIUM
LADY IN THE BOX
SIMON STIMSON
MRS. SOAMES
CONSTABLE WARREN
SI CROWELL
THREE BASEBALL PLAYERS
SAM CRAIG
JOE STODDARD

The entire play takes place in Grover's Corners,
New Hampshire.

Act I

No curtain.

No scenery.

The audience, arriving, sees an empty stage in half-light.

Presently the STAGE MANAGER, *hat on and pipe in mouth, enters and begins placing a table and three chairs downstage left, and a table and three chairs downstage right.*

He also places a low bench at the corner of what will be the Webb house, left.

"Left" and "right" are from the point of view of the actor facing the audience. "Up" is toward the back wall.

As the house lights go down he has finished setting the stage and leaning against the right proscenium pillar watches the late arrivals in the audience.

When the auditorium is in complete darkness he speaks:

STAGE MANAGER:

This play is called "Our Town." It was written by Thornton Wilder; produced and directed by A. . . . (or: produced by A. . . . ; directed by B. . . .). In it you will see Miss C. . . . ; Miss D. . . . ; Miss E. . . . ; and Mr. F. . . . ; Mr. G. . . . ;

Mr. H. . . . ; and many others. The name of the town is Grover's Corners, New Hampshire—just across the Massachusetts line: latitude 42 degrees 40 minutes; longitude 70 degrees 37 minutes. The First Act shows a day in our town. The day is May 7, 1901. The time is just before dawn.

A rooster crows.

The sky is beginning to show some streaks of light over in the East there, behind our mount'in.

The morning star always gets wonderful bright the minute before it has to go,—doesn't it?

He stares at it for a moment, then goes upstage.

Well, I'd better show you how our town lies. Up here—

That is: parallel with the back wall.

is Main Street. Way back there is the railway station; tracks go that way. Polish Town's across the tracks, and some Canuck families.

Toward the left.

Over there is the Congregational Church; across the street's the Presbyterian.

Methodist and Unitarian are over there.

Baptist is down in the holla' by the river.

Catholic Church is over beyond the tracks.

Here's the Town Hall and Post Office combined; jail's in the basement.

Bryan once made a speech from these very steps here.

Along here's a row of stores. Hitching posts and horse blocks in front of them. First automobile's going to come along in about five years—belonged to Banker Cartwright, our richest citizen . . . lives in the big white house up on the hill.

Here's the grocery store and here's Mr. Morgan's drugstore. Most everybody in town manages to look into those two stores once a day.

Public School's over yonder. High School's still farther over. Quarter of nine mornings, noontimes, and three o'clock afternoons, the hull town can hear the yelling and screaming from those schoolyards.

He approaches the table and chairs downstage right.

This is our doctor's house,—Doc Gibbs'. This is the back door.

Two arched trellises, covered with vines and flowers, are pushed out, one by each proscenium pillar.

There's some scenery for those who think they have to have scenery.

This is Mrs. Gibbs' garden. Corn . . . peas . . . beans . . . hollyhocks . . . heliotrope . . . and a lot of burdock.

Crosses the stage.

In those days our newspaper come out twice a week—the Grover's Corners *Sentinel*—and this is Editor Webb's house.

And this is Mrs. Webb's garden.

Just like Mrs. Gibbs', only it's got a lot of sunflowers, too.

He looks upward, center stage.

Right here . . .'s a big butternut tree.

He returns to his place by the right proscenium pillar and looks at the audience for a minute.

Nice town, y'know what I mean?

Nobody very remarkable ever come out of it, s'far as we know.

The earliest tombstones in the cemetery up there on the mountain say 1670–1680—they're Grovers and Cartwrights and Gibbses and Herseys—same names as are around here now.

Well, as I said: it's about dawn.

The only lights on in town are in a cottage over by the tracks where a Polish mother's just had twins. And in the Joe Crowell house, where Joe Junior's getting up so as to deliver the paper. And in the depot, where Shorty Hawkins is gettin' ready to flag the 5:45 for Boston.

A train whistle is heard. The STAGE MANAGER *takes out his watch and nods.*

Naturally, out in the country—all around—there've been lights on for some time, what with milkin's and so on. But town people sleep late.

So—another day's begun.

There's Doc Gibbs comin' down Main Street now, comin' back from that baby case. And here's his wife comin' downstairs to get breakfast.

MRS. GIBBS, *a plump, pleasant woman in the middle thirties, comes "downstairs" right. She pulls up an imaginary window shade in her kitchen and starts to make a fire in her stove.*

Doc Gibbs died in 1930. The new hospital's named after him.

Mrs. Gibbs died first—long time ago, in fact. She went out to visit her daughter, Rebecca, who married an insurance man in Canton, Ohio, and died there—pneumonia—but her body was brought back here. She's up in the cemetery there now—in with a whole mess of Gibbses and Herseys—she was Julia Hersey 'fore she married Doc Gibbs in the Congregational Church over there.

In our town we like to know the facts about everybody.

There's Mrs. Webb, coming downstairs to get her breakfast, too.

—That's Doc Gibbs. Got that call at half past one this morning.

And there comes Joe Crowell, Jr., delivering Mr. Webb's *Sentinel.*

> DR. GIBBS *has been coming along Main Street from the left. At the point where he would turn to approach his house, he stops, sets down his—imaginary—black bag, takes off his hat, and rubs his face with fatigue, using an enormous handkerchief.*

> MRS. WEBB, *a thin, serious, crisp woman, has entered her kitchen, left, tying on an apron. She goes through the motions of putting wood into a stove, lighting it, and preparing breakfast.*

> *Suddenly,* JOE CROWELL, JR., *eleven, starts down Main Street from the right, hurling imaginary newspapers into doorways.*

JOE CROWELL, JR.:
Morning, Doc Gibbs.

DR. GIBBS:
Morning, Joe.

JOE CROWELL, JR.:
Somebody been sick, Doc?

DR. GIBBS:

No. Just some twins born over in Polish Town.

JOE CROWELL, JR.:

Do you want your paper now?

DR. GIBBS:

Yes, I'll take it.—Anything serious goin' on in the world since Wednesday?

JOE CROWELL, JR.:

Yessir. My schoolteacher, Miss Foster, 's getting married to a fella over in Concord.

DR. GIBBS:

I declare.—How do you boys feel about that?

JOE CROWELL, JR.:

Well, of course, it's none of my business—but I think if a person starts out to be a teacher, she ought to stay one.

DR. GIBBS:

How's your knee, Joe?

JOE CROWELL, JR.:

Fine, Doc, I never think about it at all. Only like you said, it always tells me when it's going to rain.

DR. GIBBS:

What's it telling you today? Goin' to rain?

JOE CROWELL, JR.:

No, sir.

DR. GIBBS:

Sure?

JOE CROWELL, JR.:

Yessir.

DR. GIBBS:

Knee ever make a mistake?

JOE CROWELL, JR.:

No, sir.

JOE *goes off.* DR. GIBBS *stands reading his paper.*

STAGE MANAGER:

Want to tell you something about that boy Joe Crowell there. Joe was awful bright—graduated from high school here, head of his class. So he got a scholarship to Massachusetts Tech. Graduated head of his class there, too. It was all wrote up in the Boston paper at the time. Goin' to be a great engineer, Joe was. But the war broke out and he died in France.—All that education for nothing.

HOWIE NEWSOME:

Off left.

Giddap, Bessie! What's the matter with you today?

STAGE MANAGER:

Here comes Howie Newsome, deliverin' the milk.

HOWIE NEWSOME, *about thirty, in overalls, comes along Main Street from the left, walking beside an invisible horse and wagon and carrying an imaginary rack with milk bottles. The sound of clinking milk bottles is heard. He leaves some bottles at Mrs. Webb's trellis, then, crossing the stage to Mrs. Gibbs', he stops center to talk to Dr. Gibbs.*

HOWIE NEWSOME:

Morning, Doc.

DR. GIBBS:

Morning, Howie.

HOWIE NEWSOME:

Somebody sick?

DR. GIBBS:

Pair of twins over to Mrs. Goruslawski's.

HOWIE NEWSOME:

Twins, eh? This town's gettin' bigger every year.

DR. GIBBS:

Goin' to rain, Howie?

HOWIE NEWSOME:

No, no. Fine day—that'll burn through. Come on, Bessie.

DR. GIBBS:

Hello Bessie.

He strokes the horse, which has remained up center.

How old is she, Howie?

HOWIE NEWSOME:

Going on seventeen. Bessie's all mixed up about the route ever since the Lockharts stopped takin' their quart of milk every day. She wants to leave 'em a quart just the same— keeps scolding me the hull trip.

He reaches Mrs. Gibbs' back door. She is waiting for him.

MRS. GIBBS:

Good morning, Howie.

HOWIE NEWSOME:

Morning, Mrs. Gibbs. Doc's just comin' down the street.

MRS. GIBBS:

Is he? Seems like you're late today.

HOWIE NEWSOME:

Yes. Somep'n went wrong with the separator. Don't know what 'twas.

He passes Dr. Gibbs up center.

Doc!

DR. GIBBS:

Howie!

MRS. GIBBS:

Calling upstairs.

Children! Children! Time to get up.

HOWIE NEWSOME:

Come on, Bessie!

He goes off right.

MRS. GIBBS:

George! Rebecca!

DR. GIBBS *arrives at his back door and passes through the trellis into his house.*

MRS. GIBBS:

Everything all right, Frank?

DR. GIBBS:

Yes. I declare—easy as kittens.

MRS. GIBBS:

Bacon'll be ready in a minute. Set down and drink your coffee. You can catch a couple hours' sleep this morning, can't you?

DR. GIBBS:

Hm! . . . Mrs. Wentworth's coming at eleven. Guess I know what it's about, too. Her stummick ain't what it ought to be.

MRS. GIBBS:

All told, you won't get more'n three hours' sleep. Frank Gibbs, I don't know what's goin' to become of you. I do wish I could get you to go away someplace and take a rest. I think it would do you good.

MRS. WEBB:

Emileeee! Time to get up! Wally! Seven o'clock!

MRS. GIBBS:

I declare, you got to speak to George. Seems like something's come over him lately. He's no help to me at all. I can't even get him to cut me some wood.

DR. GIBBS:

Washing and drying his hands at the sink. MRS. GIBBS *is busy at the stove.*

Is he sassy to you?

MRS. GIBBS:

No. He just whines! All he thinks about is that baseball— George! Rebecca! You'll be late for school.

DR. GIBBS:

M-m-m . . .

MRS. GIBBS:

George!

DR. GIBBS:

George, look sharp!

GEORGE'S VOICE:

Yes, Pa!

DR. GIBBS:

As he goes off the stage.

Don't you hear your mother calling you? I guess I'll go upstairs and get forty winks.

MRS. WEBB:

Walleee! Emileee! You'll be late for school! Walleee! You wash yourself good or I'll come up and do it myself.

REBECCA GIBBS' VOICE:

Ma! What dress shall I wear?

MRS. GIBBS:

Don't make a noise. Your father's been out all night and needs his sleep. I washed and ironed the blue gingham for you special.

REBECCA:

Ma, I hate that dress.

MRS. GIBBS:

Oh, hush-up-with-you.

REBECCA:

Every day I go to school dressed like a sick turkey.

MRS. GIBBS:

Now, Rebecca, you always look *very* nice.

REBECCA:

Mama, George's throwing soap at me.

MRS. GIBBS:

I'll come and slap the both of you,—that's what I'll do.

A factory whistle sounds.

The CHILDREN *dash in and take their places at the tables. Right,* GEORGE, *about sixteen, and* REBECCA, *eleven. Left,* EMILY *and* WALLY, *same ages. They carry strapped schoolbooks.*

STAGE MANAGER:

We've got a factory in our town too—hear it? Makes blankets. Cartwrights own it and it brung 'em a fortune.

MRS. WEBB:

Children! Now I won't have it. Breakfast is just as good as any other meal and I won't have you gobbling like wolves. It'll stunt your growth,—that's a fact. Put away your book, Wally.

WALLY:

Aw, Ma! By ten o'clock I got to know all about Canada.

MRS. WEBB:

You know the rule's well as I do—no books at table. As for me, I'd rather have my children healthy than bright.

EMILY:

I'm both, Mama: you know I am. I'm the brightest girl in school for my age. I have a wonderful memory.

MRS. WEBB:

Eat your breakfast.

WALLY:

I'm bright, too, when I'm looking at my stamp collection.

MRS. GIBBS:

I'll speak to your father about it when he's rested. Seems to me twenty-five cents a week's enough for a boy your age. I declare I don't know how you spend it all.

GEORGE:

Aw, Ma,—I gotta lotta things to buy.

MRS. GIBBS:

Strawberry phosphates—that's what you spend it on.

GEORGE:

I don't see how Rebecca comes to have so much money. She has more'n a dollar.

REBECCA:

Spoon in mouth, dreamily.

I've been saving it up gradual.

MRS. GIBBS:

Well, dear, I think it's a good thing to spend some every now and then.

REBECCA:

Mama, do you know what I love most in the world—do you?—Money.

MRS. GIBBS:

Eat your breakfast.

THE CHILDREN:

Mama, there's first bell.—I gotta hurry.—I don't want any more.—I gotta hurry.

The CHILDREN *rise, seize their books and dash out through the trellises. They meet, down center, and chattering, walk to Main Street, then turn left.*

The STAGE MANAGER *goes off, unobtrusively, right.*

MRS. WEBB:

Walk fast, but you don't have to run. Wally, pull up your pants at the knee. Stand up straight, Emily.

MRS. GIBBS:

Tell Miss Foster I send her my best congratulations—can you remember that?

REBECCA:

Yes, Ma.

MRS. GIBBS:

You look real nice, Rebecca. Pick up your feet.

ALL:

Good-by.

MRS. GIBBS *fills her apron with food for the chickens and comes down to the footlights.*

MRS. GIBBS:

Here, chick, chick, chick.

No, go away, you. Go away.

Here, chick, chick, chick.

What's the matter with *you?* Fight, fight, fight,—that's all you do.

Hm . . . *you* don't belong to me. Where'd you come from?

She shakes her apron.

Oh, don't be so scared. Nobody's going to hurt you.

MRS. WEBB *is sitting on the bench by her trellis, stringing beans.*

Good morning, Myrtle. How's your cold?

MRS. WEBB:

Well, I still get that tickling feeling in my throat. I told Charles I didn't know as I'd go to choir practice tonight. Wouldn't be any use.

MRS. GIBBS:

Have you tried singing over your voice?

MRS. WEBB:

Yes, but somehow I can't do that and stay on the key. While I'm resting myself I thought I'd string some of these beans.

MRS. GIBBS:

Rolling up her sleeves as she crosses the stage for a chat.

Let me help you. Beans have been good this year.

MRS. WEBB:

I've decided to put up forty quarts if it kills me. The children say they hate 'em, but I notice they're able to get 'em down all winter.

Pause. Brief sound of chickens cackling.

MRS. GIBBS:

Now, Myrtle. I've got to tell you something, because if I don't tell somebody I'll burst.

MRS. WEBB:

Why, Julia Gibbs!

MRS. GIBBS:

Here, give me some more of those beans. Myrtle, did one of those secondhand-furniture men from Boston come to see you last Friday?

MRS. WEBB:

No-o.

MRS. GIBBS:

Well, he called on me. First I thought he was a patient wantin' to see Dr. Gibbs. 'N he wormed his way into my parlor, and, Myrtle Webb, he offered me three hundred and fifty dollars for Grandmother Wentworth's highboy, as I'm sitting here!

MRS. WEBB:

Why, Julia Gibbs!

MRS. GIBBS:

He did! That old thing! Why, it was so big I didn't know where to put it and I almost give it to Cousin Hester Wilcox.

MRS. WEBB:

Well, you're going to take it, aren't you?

MRS. GIBBS:

I don't know.

MRS. WEBB:

You don't know—three hundred and fifty dollars! What's come over you?

MRS. GIBBS:

Well, if I could get the Doctor to take the money and go away someplace on a real trip, I'd sell it like that.—Y'know, Myrtle, it's been the dream of my life to see Paris, France.— Oh, I don't know. It sounds crazy, I suppose, but for years I've been promising myself that if we ever had the chance—

MRS. WEBB:

How does the Doctor feel about it?

MRS. GIBBS:

Well, I did beat about the bush a little and said that if I got a legacy—that's the way I put it—I'd make him take me somewhere.

MRS. WEBB:

M-m-m . . . What did he say?

MRS. GIBBS:

You know how he is. I haven't heard a serious word out of him since I've known him. No, he said, it might make him discontented with Grover's Corners to go traipsin' about Europe; better let well enough alone, he says. Every two years he makes a trip to the battlefields of the Civil War and that's enough treat for anybody, he says.

MRS. WEBB:

Well, Mr. Webb just *admires* the way Dr. Gibbs knows everything about the Civil War. Mr. Webb's a good mind to give up Napoleon and move over to the Civil War, only Dr. Gibbs being one of the greatest experts in the country just makes him despair.

MRS. GIBBS:

It's a fact! Dr. Gibbs is never so happy as when he's at Antietam or Gettysburg. The times I've walked over those hills, Myrtle, stopping at every bush and pacing it all out, like we were going to buy it.

MRS. WEBB:

Well, if that secondhand man's really serious about buyin' it, Julia, you sell it. And then you'll get to see Paris, all right. Just keep droppin' hints from time to time—that's how I got to see the Atlantic Ocean, y'know.

MRS. GIBBS:

Oh, I'm sorry I mentioned it. Only it seems to me that once in your life before you die you ought to see a country where they don't talk in English and don't even want to.

The STAGE MANAGER *enters briskly from the right. He tips his hat to the ladies, who nod their heads.*

STAGE MANAGER:

Thank you, ladies. Thank you very much.

MRS. GIBBS *and* MRS. WEBB *gather up their things, return into their homes and disappear.*

Now we're going to skip a few hours.

But first we want a little more information about the town, kind of a scientific account, you might say.

So I've asked Professor Willard of our State University to sketch in a few details of our past history here.

Is Professor Willard here?

> PROFESSOR WILLARD, *a rural savant, pince-nez on a wide satin ribbon, enters from the right with some notes in his hand.*

May I introduce Professor Willard of our State University.

A few brief notes, thank you, Professor,—unfortunately our time is limited.

PROFESSOR WILLARD:

Grover's Corners . . . let me see . . . Grover's Corners lies on the old Pleistocene granite of the Appalachian range. I may say it's some of the oldest land in the world. We're very proud of that. A shelf of Devonian basalt crosses it with vestiges of Mesozoic shale, and some sandstone outcroppings; but that's all more recent: two hundred, three hundred million years old.

Some highly interesting fossils have been found . . . I may say: unique fossils . . . two miles out of town, in Silas Peckham's cow pasture. They can be seen at the museum in our University at any time—that is, at any reasonable time. Shall I read some of Professor Gruber's notes on the meteorological situation—mean precipitation, et cetera?

STAGE MANAGER:

Afraid we won't have time for that, Professor. We might have a few words on the history of man here.

PROFESSOR WILLARD:

Yes . . . anthropological data: Early Amerindian stock. Cota-hatchee tribes . . . no evidence before the tenth century of this era . . . hm . . . now entirely disappeared . . . possible traces in three families. Migration toward the end of the seventeenth century of English brachiocephalic blue-eyed stock . . . for the most part. Since then some Slav and Mediterranean—

STAGE MANAGER:

And the population, Professor Willard?

PROFESSOR WILLARD:

Within the town limits: 2,640.

STAGE MANAGER:

Just a moment, Professor.

He whispers into the professor's ear.

PROFESSOR WILLARD:

Oh, yes, indeed?—The population, *at the moment,* is 2,642. The Postal District brings in 507 more, making a total of 3,149.—Mortality and birth rates: constant.—By MacPherson's gauge: 6.032.

STAGE MANAGER:

Thank you very much, Professor. We're all very much obliged to you, I'm sure.

PROFESSOR WILLARD:

Not at all, sir; not at all.

STAGE MANAGER:

This way, Professor, and thank you again.

Exit PROFESSOR WILLARD.

Now the political and social report: Editor Webb.—Oh, Mr. Webb?

MRS. WEBB *appears at her back door.*

MRS. WEBB:
He'll be here in a minute. . . . He just cut his hand while he was eatin' an apple.

STAGE MANAGER:
Thank you, Mrs. Webb.

MRS. WEBB:
Charles! Everybody's waitin'.

Exit MRS. WEBB.

STAGE MANAGER:
Mr. Webb is Publisher and Editor of the Grover's Corners *Sentinel.* That's our local paper, y'know.

MR. WEBB *enters from his house, pulling on his coat. His finger is bound in a handkerchief.*

MR. WEBB:
Well . . . I don't have to tell you that we're run here by a Board of Selectmen.—All males vote at the age of twenty-one. Women vote indirect. We're lower middle class: sprinkling of professional men . . . ten per cent illiterate laborers. Politically, we're eighty-six per cent Republicans; six per cent Democrats; four per cent Socialists; rest, indifferent.

Religiously, we're eighty-five per cent Protestants; twelve per cent Catholics; rest, indifferent.

STAGE MANAGER:
Have you any comments, Mr. Webb?

MR. WEBB:
Very ordinary town, if you ask me. Little better behaved than most. Probably a lot duller.

But our young people here seem to like it well enough. Ninety per cent of 'em graduating from high school settle down right here to live—even when they've been away to college.

STAGE MANAGER:

Now, is there anyone in the audience who would like to ask Editor Webb anything about the town?

WOMAN IN THE BALCONY:

Is there much drinking in Grover's Corners?

MR. WEBB:

Well, ma'am, I wouldn't know what you'd call *much*. Satiddy nights the farmhands meet down in Ellery Greenough's stable and holler some. We've got one or two town drunks, but they're always having remorses every time an evangelist comes to town. No, ma'am, I'd say likker ain't a regular thing in the home here, except in the medicine chest. Right good for snake bite, y'know—always was.

BELLIGERENT MAN AT BACK OF AUDITORIUM:

Is there no one in town aware of—

STAGE MANAGER:

Come forward, will you, where we can all hear you—What were you saying?

BELLIGERENT MAN:

Is there no one in town aware of social injustice and indus-trial inequality?

MR. WEBB:

Oh, yes, everybody is—somethin' terrible. Seems like they spend most of their time talking about who's rich and who's poor.

BELLIGERENT MAN:

Then why don't they do something about it?

He withdraws without waiting for an answer.

MR. WEBB:

Well, I dunno. . . . I guess we're all hunting like everybody else for a way the diligent and sensible can rise to the top and the lazy and quarrelsome can sink to the bottom. But it ain't easy to find. Meanwhile, we do all we can to help those that can't help themselves and those that can we leave alone.—Are there any other questions?

LADY IN A BOX:

Oh, Mr. Webb? Mr. Webb, is there any culture or love of beauty in Grover's Corners?

MR. WEBB:

Well, ma'am, there ain't much—not in the sense you mean. Come to think of it, there's some girls that play the piano at High School Commencement; but they ain't happy about it. No, ma'am, there isn't much culture; but maybe this is the place to tell you that we've got a lot of pleasures of a kind here: we like the sun comin' up over the mountain in the morning, and we all notice a good deal about the birds. We pay a lot of attention to them. And we watch the change of the seasons; yes, everybody knows about them. But those other things—you're right, ma'am,—there ain't much.— *Robinson Crusoe* and the Bible; and Handel's "Largo," we all know that; and Whistler's "Mother"—those are just about as far as we go.

LADY IN A BOX:

So I thought. Thank you, Mr. Webb.

STAGE MANAGER:

Thank you, Mr. Webb.

MR. WEBB *retires.*

Now, we'll go back to the town. It's early afternoon. All 2,642 have had their dinners and all the dishes have been washed.

MR. WEBB, having removed his coat, returns and starts pushing a lawn mower to and fro beside his house.

There's an early-afternoon calm in our town: a buzzin' and a hummin' from the school buildings; only a few buggies on Main Street—the horses dozing at the hitching posts; you all remember what it's like. Doc Gibbs is in his office, tapping people and making them say "ah." Mr. Webb's cuttin' his lawn over there; one man in ten thinks it's a privilege to push his own lawn mower.

No, sir. It's later than I thought. There are the children coming home from school already.

Shrill girls' voices are heard, off left. EMILY *comes along Main Street, carrying some books. There are some signs that she is imagining herself to be a lady of startling elegance.*

EMILY:

I *can't*, Lois. I've got to go home and help my mother. I *promised*.

MR. WEBB:

Emily, walk simply. Who do you think you are today?

EMILY:

Papa, you're terrible. One minute you tell me to stand up straight and the next minute you call me names. I just don't listen to you.

She gives him an abrupt kiss.

MR. WEBB:

Golly, I never got a kiss from such a great lady before.

He goes out of sight. EMILY *leans over and picks some flowers by the gate of her house.*

GEORGE GIBBS *comes careening down Main Street. He is throwing a ball up to dizzying heights, and waiting to catch it again. This sometimes requires his taking six steps backward. He bumps into an* OLD LADY *invisible to us.*

GEORGE:
Excuse me, Mrs. Forrest.

STAGE MANAGER:
As Mrs. Forrest.

Go out and play in the fields, young man. You got no business playing baseball on Main Street.

GEORGE:
Awfully sorry, Mrs. Forrest.—Hello, Emily.

EMILY:
H'lo.

GEORGE:
You made a fine speech in class.

EMILY:
Well . . . I was really ready to make a speech about the Monroe Doctrine, but at the last minute Miss Corcoran made me talk about the Louisiana Purchase instead. I worked an awful long time on both of them.

GEORGE:
Gee, it's funny, Emily. From my window up there I can just see your head nights when you're doing your homework over in your room.

EMILY:

Why, can you?

GEORGE:

You certainly do stick to it, Emily. I don't see how you can sit still that long. I guess you like school.

EMILY:

Well, I always feel it's something you have to go through.

GEORGE:

Yeah.

EMILY:

I don't mind it really. It passes the time.

GEORGE:

Yeah.—Emily, what do you think? We might work out a kinda telegraph from your window to mine; and once in a while you could give me a kinda hint or two about one of those algebra problems. I don't mean the answers, Emily, of course not . . . just some little hint . . .

EMILY:

Oh, I think *hints* are allowed.—So—ah—if you get stuck, George, you whistle to me; and I'll give you some hints.

GEORGE:

Emily, you're just naturally bright, I guess.

EMILY:

I figure that it's just the way a person's born.

GEORGE:

Yeah. But, you see, I want to be a farmer, and my Uncle Luke says whenever I'm ready I can come over and work on his farm and if I'm any good I can just gradually have it.

EMILY:

You mean the house and everything?

Enter MRS. WEBB *with a large bowl and sits on the bench by her trellis.*

GEORGE:

Yeah. Well, thanks . . . I better be getting out to the baseball field. Thanks for the talk, Emily.—Good afternoon, Mrs. Webb.

MRS. WEBB:

Good afternoon, George.

GEORGE:

So long, Emily.

EMILY:

So long, George.

MRS. WEBB:

Emily, come and help me string these beans for the winter. George Gibbs let himself have a real conversation, didn't he? Why, he's growing up. How old would George be?

EMILY:

I don't know.

MRS. WEBB:

Let's see. He must be almost sixteen.

EMILY:

Mama, I made a speech in class today and I was very good.

MRS. WEBB:

You must recite it to your father at supper. What was it about?

EMILY:

The Louisiana Purchase. It was like silk off a spool. I'm going to make speeches all my life.—Mama, are these big enough?

MRS. WEBB:

Try and get them a little bigger if you can.

EMILY:

Mama, will you answer me a question, serious?

MRS. WEBB:

Seriously, dear—not serious.

EMILY:

Seriously,—will you?

MRS. WEBB:

Of course, I will.

EMILY:

Mama, am I good looking?

MRS. WEBB:

Yes, of course you are. All my children have got good features; I'd be ashamed if they hadn't.

EMILY:

Oh, Mama, that's not what I mean. What I mean is: am I *pretty*?

MRS. WEBB:

I've already told you, yes. Now that's enough of that. You have a nice young pretty face. I never heard of such foolishness.

EMILY:

Oh, Mama, you never tell us the truth about anything.

MRS. WEBB:

I *am* telling you the truth.

EMILY:

Mama, were *you* pretty?

MRS. WEBB:

Yes, I was, if I do say it. I was the prettiest girl in town next to Mamie Cartwright.

EMILY:

But, Mama, you've got to say *some*thing about me. Am I pretty enough . . . to get anybody . . . to get people interested in me?

MRS. WEBB:

Emily, you make me tired. Now stop it. You're pretty enough for all normal purposes.—Come along now and bring that bowl with you.

EMILY:

Oh, Mama, you're no help at all.

STAGE MANAGER:

Thank you. Thank you! That'll do. We'll have to interrupt again here. Thank you, Mrs. Webb; thank you, Emily.

MRS. WEBB *and* EMILY *withdraw.*

There are some more things we want to explore about this town.

He comes to the center of the stage. During the following speech the lights gradually dim to darkness, leaving only a spot on him.

I think this is a good time to tell you that the Cartwright interests have just begun building a new bank in Grover's Corners—had to go to Vermont for the marble, sorry to say. And they've asked a friend of mine what they should put in the cornerstone for people to dig up . . . a thousand years from now. . . . Of course, they've put in a copy of the *New York Times* and a copy of Mr. Webb's *Sentinel*. . . . We're kind of interested in this because some scientific fellas have found a way of painting all that reading matter with a glue—a silicate glue—that'll make it keep a thousand—two thousand years.

We're putting in a Bible . . . and the Constitution of the United States—and a copy of William Shakespeare's plays. What do you say, folks? What do you think?

Y'know—Babylon once had two million people in it, and all we know about 'em is the names of the kings and some copies of wheat contracts . . . and contracts for the sale of slaves. Yet every night all those families sat down to supper, and the father came home from his work, and the smoke went up the chimney,—same as here. And even in Greece and Rome, all we know about the *real* life of the people is what we can piece together out of the joking poems and the comedies they wrote for the theatre back then.

So I'm going to have a copy of this play put in the cornerstone and the people a thousand years from now'll know a few simple facts about us—more than the Treaty of Versailles and the Lindbergh flight.

See what I mean?

So—people a thousand years from now—this is the way we were in the provinces north of New York at the beginning of the twentieth century.—This is the way we were: in our growing up and in our marrying and in our living and in our dying.

A choir partially concealed in the orchestra pit has begun singing "Blessed Be the Tie That Binds."

SIMON STIMSON *stands directing them.*

Two ladders have been pushed onto the stage; they serve as indication of the second story in the Gibbs and Webb houses. GEORGE *and* EMILY *mount them, and apply themselves to their schoolwork.*

DR. GIBBS *has entered and is seated in his kitchen reading.*

Well!—good deal of time's gone by. It's evening.

You can hear choir practice going on in the Congregational Church.

The children are at home doing their schoolwork.

The day's running down like a tired clock.

SIMON STIMSON:
Now look here, everybody. Music come into the world to give pleasure.—Softer! Softer! Get it out of your heads that music's only good when it's loud. You leave loudness to the Methodists. You couldn't beat 'em, even if you wanted to. Now again. Tenors!

GEORGE:
Hssst! Emily!

EMILY:
Hello.

GEORGE:
Hello!

EMILY:
I can't work at all. The moonlight's so *terrible.*

GEORGE:
Emily, did you get the third problem?

EMILY:

Which?

GEORGE:

The *third*?

EMILY:

Why, yes, George—that's the easiest of them all.

GEORGE:

I don't see it. Emily, can you give me a hint?

EMILY:

I'll tell you one thing: the answer's in yards.

GEORGE:

!!! In yards? How do you mean?

EMILY:

In *square* yards.

GEORGE:

Oh . . . in square yards.

EMILY:

Yes, George, don't you see?

GEORGE:

Yeah.

EMILY:

In square yards of *wallpaper*.

GEORGE:

Wallpaper,—oh, I see. Thanks a lot, Emily.

EMILY:

You're welcome. My, isn't the moonlight *terrible*? And choir
practice going on.—I think if you hold your breath you can
hear the train all the way to Contoocook. Hear it?

GEORGE:

M-m-m—What do you know!

EMILY:

Well, I guess I better go back and try to work.

GEORGE:

Good night, Emily. And thanks.

EMILY:

Good night, George.

SIMON STIMSON:

Before I forget it: how many of you will be able to come in Tuesday afternoon and sing at Fred Hersey's wedding?— show your hands. That'll be fine; that'll be right nice. We'll do the same music we did for Jane Trowbridge's last month.

—Now we'll do: "Art Thou Weary; Art Thou Languid?" It's a question, ladies and gentlemen, make it talk. Ready.

DR. GIBBS:

Oh, George, can you come down a minute?

GEORGE:

Yes, Pa.

He descends the ladder.

DR. GIBBS:

Make yourself comfortable, George; I'll only keep you a minute. George, how old are you?

GEORGE:

I? I'm sixteen, almost seventeen.

DR. GIBBS:

What do you want to do after school's over?

GEORGE:

Why, you know, Pa. I want to be a farmer on Uncle Luke's farm.

DR. GIBBS:

You'll be willing, will you, to get up early and milk and feed the stock . . . and you'll be able to hoe and hay all day?

GEORGE:

Sure, I will. What are you . . . what do you mean, Pa?

DR. GIBBS:

Well, George, while I was in my office today I heard a funny sound . . . and what do you think it was? It was your mother chopping wood. There you see your mother—getting up early; cooking meals all day long; washing and ironing;—and still she has to go out in the back yard and chop wood. I suppose she just got tired of asking you. She just gave up and decided it was easier to do it herself. And you eat her meals, and put on the clothes she keeps nice for you, and you run off and play baseball,—like she's some hired girl we keep around the house but that we don't like very much. Well, I knew all I had to do was call your attention to it. Here's a handkerchief, son. George, I've decided to raise your spending money twenty-five cents a week. Not, of course, for chopping wood for your mother, because that's a present you give her, but because you're getting older—and I imagine there are lots of things you must find to do with it.

GEORGE:

Thanks, Pa.

DR. GIBBS:

Let's see—tomorrow's your payday. You can count on it— Hmm. Probably Rebecca'll feel she ought to have some more too. Wonder what could have happened to your mother. Choir practice never was as late as this before.

GEORGE:

It's only half past eight, Pa.

DR. GIBBS:

I don't know why she's in that old choir. She hasn't any more voice than an old crow. . . . Traipsin' around the streets at this hour of the night . . . Just about time you retired, don't you think?

GEORGE:

Yes, Pa.

GEORGE *mounts to his place on the ladder.*

Laughter and good nights can be heard on stage left and presently MRS. GIBBS, MRS. SOAMES *and* MRS. WEBB *come down Main Street. When they arrive at the corner of the stage they stop.*

MRS. SOAMES:

Good night, Martha. Good night, Mr. Foster.

MRS. WEBB:

I'll tell Mr. Webb; I *know* he'll want to put it in the paper.

MRS. GIBBS:

My, it's late!

MRS. SOAMES:

Good night, Irma.

MRS. GIBBS:

Real nice choir practice, wa'n't it? Myrtle Webb! Look at that moon, will you! Tsk-tsk-tsk. Potato weather, for sure.

They are silent a moment, gazing up at the moon.

MRS. SOAMES:

Naturally I didn't want to say a word about it in front of those others, but now we're alone—really, it's the worst scandal that ever was in this town!

MRS. GIBBS:

What?

MRS. SOAMES:

Simon Stimson!

MRS. GIBBS:

Now, Louella!

MRS. SOAMES:

But, Julia! To have the organist of a church *drink* and *drunk* year after year. You know he was drunk tonight.

MRS. GIBBS:

Now, Louella! We all know about Mr. Stimson, and we all know about the troubles he's been through, and Dr. Ferguson knows too, and if Dr. Ferguson keeps him on there in his job the only thing the rest of us can do is just not to notice it.

MRS. SOAMES:

Not to notice it! But it's getting worse.

MRS. WEBB:

No, it isn't, Louella. It's getting better. I've been in that choir twice as long as you have. It doesn't happen anywhere near so often. . . . My, I hate to go to bed on a night like this.—I better hurry. Those children'll be sitting up till all hours. Good night, Louella.

They all exchange good nights. She hurries downstage, enters her house and disappears.

MRS. GIBBS:

Can you get home safe, Louella?

MRS. SOAMES:

It's as bright as day. I can see Mr. Soames scowling at the window now. You'd think we'd been to a dance the way the menfolk carry on.

More good nights. MRS. GIBBS *arrives at her home and passes through the trellis into the kitchen.*

MRS. GIBBS:

Well, we had a real good time.

DR. GIBBS:

You're late enough.

MRS. GIBBS:

Why, Frank, it ain't any later 'n usual.

DR. GIBBS:

And you stopping at the corner to gossip with a lot of hens.

MRS. GIBBS:

Now, Frank, don't be grouchy. Come out and smell the heliotrope in the moonlight.

They stroll out arm in arm along the footlights.

Isn't that wonderful? What did you do all the time I was away?

DR. GIBBS:

Oh, I read—as usual. What were the girls gossiping about tonight?

MRS. GIBBS:

Well, believe me, Frank—there is something to gossip about.

DR. GIBBS:

Hmm! Simon Stimson far gone, was he?

MRS. GIBBS:

Worst I've ever seen him. How'll that end, Frank? Dr. Ferguson can't forgive him forever.

DR. GIBBS:

I guess I know more about Simon Stimson's affairs than anybody in this town. Some people ain't made for small-town life. I don't know how that'll end; but there's nothing we can do but just leave it alone. Come, get in.

MRS. GIBBS:

No, not yet . . . Frank, I'm worried about you.

DR. GIBBS:

What are you worried about?

MRS. GIBBS:

I think it's my duty to make plans for you to get a real rest and change. And if I get that legacy, well, I'm going to insist on it.

DR. GIBBS:

Now, Julia, there's no sense in going over that again.

MRS. GIBBS:

Frank, you're just *unreasonable!*

DR. GIBBS:

Starting into the house.

Come on, Julia, it's getting late. First thing you know you'll catch cold. I gave George a piece of my mind tonight.

I reckon you'll have your wood chopped for a while anyway. No, no, start getting upstairs.

MRS. GIBBS:

Oh, dear. There's always so many things to pick up, seems like. You know, Frank, Mrs. Fairchild always locks her front door every night. All those people up that part of town do.

DR. GIBBS:

Blowing out the lamp.

They're all getting citified, that's the trouble with them. They haven't got nothing fit to burgle and everybody knows it.

They disappear.

REBECCA *climbs up the ladder beside* GEORGE.

GEORGE:

Get out, Rebecca. There's only room for one at this window. You're always spoiling everything.

REBECCA:

Well, let me look just a minute.

GEORGE:

Use your own window.

REBECCA:

I did, but there's no moon there. . . . George, do you know what I think, do you? I think maybe the moon's getting nearer and nearer and there'll be a big 'splosion.

GEORGE:

Rebecca, you don't know anything. If the moon were getting nearer, the guys that sit up all night with telescopes would see it first and they'd tell about it, and it'd be in all the newspapers.

REBECCA:

George, is the moon shining on South America, Canada and half the whole world?

GEORGE:

Well—prob'ly is.

The STAGE MANAGER *strolls on.*

Pause. The sound of crickets is heard.

STAGE MANAGER:

Nine thirty. Most of the lights are out. No, there's Constable Warren trying a few doors on Main Street. And here comes Editor Webb, after putting his newspaper to bed.

MR. WARREN, *an elderly policeman, comes along Main Street from the right,* MR. WEBB *from the left.*

MR. WEBB:

Good evening, Bill.

CONSTABLE WARREN:

Evenin', Mr. Webb.

MR. WEBB:

Quite a moon!

CONSTABLE WARREN:

Yepp.

MR. WEBB:

All quiet tonight?

CONSTABLE WARREN:

Simon Stimson is rollin' around a little. Just saw his wife movin' out to hunt for him so I looked the other way—there he is now.

SIMON STIMSON *comes down Main Street from the left, only a trace of unsteadiness in his walk.*

MR. WEBB:

Good evening, Simon . . . Town seems to have settled down for the night pretty well. . . .

SIMON STIMSON *comes up to him and pauses a moment and stares at him, swaying slightly.*

Good evening . . . Yes, most of the town's settled down for the night, Simon. . . . I guess we better do the same. Can I walk along a ways with you?

SIMON STIMSON *continues on his way without a word and disappears at the right.*

Good night.

CONSTABLE WARREN:

I don't know how that's goin' to end, Mr. Webb.

MR. WEBB:

Well, he's seen a peck of trouble, one thing after another. . . . Oh, Bill . . . if you see my boy smoking cigarettes, just give him a word, will you? He thinks a lot of you, Bill.

CONSTABLE WARREN:

I don't think he smokes no cigarettes, Mr. Webb. Leastways, not more'n two or three a year.

MR. WEBB:

Hm . . . I hope not.—Well, good night, Bill.

CONSTABLE WARREN:

Good night, Mr. Webb.

Exit.

MR. WEBB:

Who's that up there? Is that you, Myrtle?

EMILY:

No, it's me, Papa.

MR. WEBB:

Why aren't you in bed?

EMILY:

I don't know. I just can't sleep yet, Papa. The moonlight's so *won*-derful. And the smell of Mrs. Gibbs' heliotrope. Can you smell it?

MR. WEBB:

Hm . . . Yes. Haven't any troubles on your mind, have you, Emily?

EMILY:

Troubles, Papa? *No.*

MR. WEBB:

Well, enjoy yourself, but don't let your mother catch you. Good night, Emily.

EMILY:

Good night, Papa.

MR. WEBB *crosses into the house, whistling "Blessed Be the Tie That Binds" and disappears.*

REBECCA:

I never told you about that letter Jane Crofut got from her minister when she was sick. He wrote Jane a letter and on the envelope the address was like this: It said: Jane Crofut; The Crofut Farm; Grover's Corners; Sutton County; New Hampshire; United States of America.

GEORGE:

What's funny about that?

REBECCA:

But listen, it's not finished: the United States of America; Continent of North America; Western Hemisphere; the Earth; the Solar System; the Universe; the Mind of God— that's what it said on the envelope.

GEORGE:

What do you know!

REBECCA:

And the postman brought it just the same.

GEORGE:

What do you know!

STAGE MANAGER:

That's the end of the First Act, friends. You can go and smoke now, those that smoke.

—m—

Act II

The tables and chairs of the two kitchens are still on the stage.
  The ladders and the small bench have been withdrawn.
    The STAGE MANAGER *has been at his accustomed place watching the audience return to its seats.*

STAGE MANAGER:
Three years have gone by.

Yes, the sun's come up over a thousand times.

Summers and winters have cracked the mountains a little bit more and the rains have brought down some of the dirt.

Some babies that weren't even born before have begun talking regular sentences already; and a number of people who thought they were right young and spry have noticed that they can't bound up a flight of stairs like they used to, without their heart fluttering a little.

All that can happen in a thousand days.

Nature's been pushing and contriving in other ways, too: a number of young people fell in love and got married.

Yes, the mountain got bit away a few fractions of an inch; millions of gallons of water went by the mill; and here and there a new home was set up under a roof.

Almost everybody in the world gets married,—you know what I mean? In our town there aren't hardly any exceptions. Most everybody in the world climbs into their graves married.

The First Act was called the Daily Life. This act is called Love and Marriage. There's another act coming after this: I reckon you can guess what that's about.

So:

It's three years later. It's 1904.

It's July 7th, just after High School Commencement.

That's the time most of our young people jump up and get married.

Soon as they've passed their last examinations in solid geometry and Cicero's Orations, looks like they suddenly feel themselves fit to be married.

It's early morning. Only this time it's been raining. It's been pouring and thundering.

Mrs. Gibbs' garden, and Mrs. Webb's here: drenched.

All those bean poles and pea vines: drenched.

All yesterday over there on Main Street, the rain looked like curtains being blown along.

Hm . . . it may begin again any minute.

There! You can hear the 5:45 for Boston.

MRS. GIBBS *and* MRS. WEBB *enter their kitchens and start the day as in the First Act.*

And there's Mrs. Gibbs and Mrs. Webb come down to make breakfast, just as though it were an ordinary day. I don't have to point out to the women in my audience that those ladies they see before them, both of those ladies cooked three meals a day—one of 'em for twenty years, the other for forty—and no summer vacation. They brought up two children apiece, washed, cleaned the house,—and *never a nervous breakdown.*

It's like what one of those Middle West poets said: You've got to love life to have life, and you've got to have life to love life. . . . It's what they call a vicious circle.

HOWIE NEWSOME:
Off stage left.

Giddap, Bessie!

STAGE MANAGER:
Here comes Howie Newsome delivering the milk. And there's Si Crowell delivering the papers like his brother before him.

SI CROWELL *has entered hurling imaginary newspapers into doorways;* HOWIE NEWSOME *has come along Main Street with Bessie.*

SI CROWELL:
Morning, Howie.

HOWIE NEWSOME:
Morning, Si.—Anything in the papers I ought to know?

SI CROWELL:
Nothing much, except we're losing about the best baseball pitcher Grover's Corners ever had—George Gibbs.

HOWIE NEWSOME:

Reckon he is.

SI CROWELL:

He could hit and run bases, too.

HOWIE NEWSOME:

Yep. Mighty fine ball player.—Whoa! Bessie! I guess I can stop and talk if I've a mind to!

SI CROWELL:

I don't see how he could give up a thing like that just to get married. Would you, Howie?

HOWIE NEWSOME:

Can't tell, Si. Never had no talent that way.

CONSTABLE WARREN *enters. They exchange good mornings.*

You're up early, Bill.

CONSTABLE WARREN:

Seein' if there's anything I can do to prevent a flood. River's been risin' all night.

HOWIE NEWSOME:

Si Crowell's all worked up here about George Gibbs' retiring from baseball.

CONSTABLE WARREN:

Yes, sir; that's the way it goes. Back in '84 we had a player, Si—even George Gibbs couldn't touch him. Name of Hank Todd. Went down to Maine and become a parson. Wonderful ball player.—Howie, how does the weather look to you?

HOWIE NEWSOME:

Oh, 'tain't bad. Think maybe it'll clear up for good.

CONSTABLE WARREN *and* SI CROWELL *continue on their way.*

HOWIE NEWSOME *brings the milk first to Mrs. Gibbs' house. She meets him by the trellis.*

MRS. GIBBS:

Good morning, Howie. Do you think it's going to rain again?

HOWIE NEWSOME:

Morning, Mrs. Gibbs. It rained so heavy, I think maybe it'll clear up.

MRS. GIBBS:

Certainly hope it will.

HOWIE NEWSOME:

How much did you want today?

MRS. GIBBS:

I'm going to have a houseful of relations, Howie. Looks to me like I'll need three-a-milk and two-a-cream.

HOWIE NEWSOME:

My wife says to tell you we both hope they'll be very happy, Mrs. Gibbs. Know they *will*.

MRS. GIBBS:

Thanks a lot, Howie. Tell your wife I hope she gits there to the wedding.

HOWIE NEWSOME:

Yes, she'll be there; she'll be there if she kin.

HOWIE NEWSOME *crosses to Mrs. Webb's house.*

Morning, Mrs. Webb.

MRS. WEBB:

Oh, good morning, Mr. Newsome. I told you four quarts of milk, but I hope you can spare me another.

HOWIE NEWSOME:

Yes'm . . . and the two of cream.

MRS. WEBB:

Will it start raining again, Mr. Newsome?

HOWIE NEWSOME:

Well. Just sayin' to Mrs. Gibbs as how it may lighten up. Mrs. Newsome told me to tell you as how we hope they'll both be very happy, Mrs. Webb. Know they *will*.

MRS. WEBB:

Thank you, and thank Mrs. Newsome and we're counting on seeing you at the wedding.

HOWIE NEWSOME:

Yes, Mrs. Webb. We hope to git there. Couldn't miss that. Come on, Bessie.

Exit HOWIE NEWSOME.

DR. GIBBS *descends in shirt sleeves, and sits down at his break-fast table.*

DR. GIBBS:

Well, Ma, the day has come. You're losin' one of your chicks.

MRS. GIBBS:

Frank Gibbs, don't you say another word. I feel like crying every minute. Sit down and drink your coffee.

DR. GIBBS:

The groom's up shaving himself—only there ain't an awful lot to shave. Whistling and singing, like he's glad to leave us.—Every now and then he says "I do" to the mirror, but it don't sound convincing to me.

MRS. GIBBS:

I declare, Frank, I don't know how he'll get along. I've arranged his clothes and seen to it he's put warm things on,—Frank! they're too *young*. Emily won't think of such things. He'll catch his death of cold within a week.

DR. GIBBS:

I was remembering my wedding morning, Julia.

MRS. GIBBS:

Now don't start that, Frank Gibbs.

DR. GIBBS:

I was the scaredest young fella in the State of New Hampshire. I thought I'd make a mistake for sure. And when I saw you comin' down that aisle I thought you were the prettiest girl I'd ever seen, but the only trouble was that I'd never seen you before. There I was in the Congregational Church marryin' a total stranger.

MRS. GIBBS:

And how do you think I felt!—Frank, weddings are perfectly awful things. Farces,—that's what they are!

She puts a plate before him.

Here, I've made something for you.

DR. GIBBS:

Why, Julia Hersey—French toast!

MRS. GIBBS:

'Tain't hard to make and I had to do *some*thing.

Pause. DR. GIBBS *pours on the syrup.*

DR. GIBBS:

How'd you sleep last night, Julia?

MRS. GIBBS:

Well, I heard a lot of the hours struck off.

DR. GIBBS:

Ye-e-s! I get a shock every time I think of George setting out to be a family man—that great gangling thing!—I tell you Julia, there's nothing so terrifying in the world as a *son*. The relation of father and son is the darndest, awkwardest—

MRS. GIBBS:

Well, mother and daughter's no picnic, let me tell you.

DR. GIBBS:

They'll have a lot of troubles, I suppose, but that's none of our business. Everybody has a right to their own troubles.

MRS. GIBBS:

At the table, drinking her coffee, meditatively.

Yes . . . people are meant to go through life two by two. 'Tain't natural to be lonesome.

Pause. DR. GIBBS *starts laughing.*

DR. GIBBS:

Julia, do you know one of the things I was scared of when I married you?

MRS. GIBBS:

Oh, go along with you!

DR. GIBBS:

I was afraid we wouldn't have material for conversation more'n'd last us a few weeks.

Both laugh.

I was afraid we'd run out and eat our meals in silence, that's a fact.—Well, you and I been conversing for twenty years now without any noticeable barren spells.

MRS. GIBBS:

Well,—good weather, bad weather—'tain't very choice, but I always find something to say.

She goes to the foot of the stairs.

Did you hear Rebecca stirring around upstairs?

DR. GIBBS:

No. Only day of the year Rebecca hasn't been managing everybody's business up there. She's hiding in her room.—I got the impression she's crying.

MRS. GIBBS:

Lord's sakes!—This has got to stop.—Rebecca! Rebecca! Come and get your breakfast.

GEORGE *comes rattling down the stairs, very brisk.*

GEORGE:

Good morning, everybody. Only five more hours to live.

Makes the gesture of cutting his throat, and a loud "k-k-k," and starts through the trellis.

MRS. GIBBS:

George Gibbs, where are you going?

GEORGE:

Just stepping across the grass to see my girl.

MRS. GIBBS:

Now, George! You put on your overshoes. It's raining torrents. You don't go out of this house without you're prepared for it.

GEORGE:

Aw, Ma. It's just a *step!*

MRS. GIBBS:

George! You'll catch your death of cold and cough all through the service.

DR. GIBBS:

George, do as your mother tells you!

DR. GIBBS *goes upstairs.*

GEORGE *returns reluctantly to the kitchen and pantomimes putting on overshoes.*

MRS. GIBBS:

From tomorrow on you can kill yourself in all weathers, but while you're in my house you'll live wisely, thank you.—Maybe Mrs. Webb isn't used to callers at seven in the morning.—Here, take a cup of coffee first.

GEORGE:

Be back in a minute.

He crosses the stage, leaping over the puddles.

Good morning, Mother Webb.

MRS. WEBB:

Goodness! You frightened me!—Now, George, you can come in a minute out of the wet, but you know I can't ask you in.

GEORGE:

Why not—?

MRS. WEBB:

George, you know 's well as I do: the groom can't see his bride on his wedding day, not until he sees her in church.

GEORGE:

Aw!—that's just a superstition.—Good morning, Mr. Webb.

Enter MR. WEBB.

MR. WEBB:

Good morning, George.

GEORGE:

Mr. Webb, you don't believe in that superstition, do you?

MR. WEBB:

There's a lot of common sense in some superstitions, George.

He sits at the table, facing right.

MRS. WEBB:

Millions have folla'd it, George, and you don't want to be the first to fly in the face of custom.

GEORGE:

How is Emily?

MRS. WEBB:

She hasn't waked up yet. I haven't heard a sound out of her.

GEORGE:

Emily's *asleep!!!*

MRS. WEBB:

No wonder! We were up 'til all hours, sewing and packing. Now I'll tell you what I'll do; you set down here a minute with Mr. Webb and drink this cup of coffee; and I'll go upstairs and see she doesn't come down and surprise you. There's some bacon, too; but don't be long about it.

Exit MRS. WEBB.

Embarrassed silence.

MR. WEBB *dunks doughnuts in his coffee.*

More silence.

MR. WEBB:
Suddenly and loudly.

Well, George, how are you?

GEORGE:
Startled, choking over his coffee.

Oh, fine, I'm fine.

Pause.

Mr. Webb, what sense could there be in a superstition like that?

MR. WEBB:
Well, you see,—on her wedding morning a girl's head's apt to be full of . . . clothes and one thing and another. Don't you think that's probably it?

GEORGE:
Ye-e-s. I never thought of that.

MR. WEBB:
A girl's apt to be a mite nervous on her wedding day.

Pause.

GEORGE:
I wish a fellow could get married without all that marching up and down.

MR. WEBB:
Every man that's ever lived has felt that way about it, George; but it hasn't been any use. It's the womenfolk who've built

up weddings, my boy. For a while now the women have it all their own. A man looks pretty small at a wedding, George. All those good women standing shoulder to shoulder making sure that the knot's tied in a mighty public way.

GEORGE:

But . . . you *believe* in it, don't you, Mr. Webb?

MR. WEBB:

With alacrity.

Oh, yes; *oh, yes.* Don't you misunderstand me, my boy. Marriage is a wonderful thing,—wonderful thing. And don't you forget that, George.

GEORGE:

No, sir.—Mr. Webb, how old were you when you got married?

MR. WEBB:

Well, you see: I'd been to college and I'd taken a little time to get settled. But Mrs. Webb—she wasn't much older than what Emily is. Oh, age hasn't much to do with it, George,— not compared with . . . uh . . . other things.

GEORGE:

What were you going to say, Mr. Webb?

MR. WEBB:

Oh, I don't know.—Was I going to say something?

Pause.

George, I was thinking the other night of some advice my father gave me when I got married. Charles, he said, Charles, start out early showing who's boss, he said. Best thing to do is to give an order, even if it don't make sense; just so she'll learn to obey. And he said: if anything about your wife irritates you—her conversation, or anything—just get up and leave the house. That'll make it clear to her, he said. And, oh, yes! he said never, *never* let your wife know how much money you have, never.

GEORGE:

Well, Mr. Webb . . . I don't think I could . . .

MR. WEBB:

So I took the opposite of my father's advice and I've been happy ever since. And let that be a lesson to you, George, never to ask advice on personal matters.—George, are you going to raise chickens on your farm?

GEORGE:

What?

MR. WEBB:

Are you going to raise chickens on your farm?

GEORGE:

Uncle Luke's never been much interested, but I thought—

MR. WEBB:

A book came into my office the other day, George, on the Philo System of raising chickens. I want you to read it. I'm thinking of beginning in a small way in the back yard, and I'm going to put an incubator in the cellar—

Enter MRS. WEBB.

MRS. WEBB:

Charles, are you talking about that old incubator again? I thought you two'd be talking about things worth while.

MR. WEBB:

Bitingly.

Well, Myrtle, if you want to give the boy some good advice, I'll go upstairs and leave you alone with him.

MRS. WEBB:

Pulling GEORGE *up.*

George, Emily's got to come downstairs and eat her breakfast. She sends you her love but she doesn't want to lay eyes on you. Good-by.

GEORGE:

Good-by.

GEORGE *crosses the stage to his own home, bewildered and crestfallen. He slowly dodges a puddle and disappears into his house.*

MR. WEBB:

Myrtle, I guess you don't know about that older superstition.

MRS. WEBB:

What do you mean, Charles?

MR. WEBB:

Since the cave men: no bridegroom should see his father-in-law on the day of the wedding, or near it. Now remember that.

Both leave the stage.

STAGE MANAGER:

Thank you very much, Mr. and Mrs. Webb.—Now I have to interrupt again here. You see, we want to know how all this began—this wedding, this plan to spend a lifetime together. I'm awfully interested in how big things like that begin.

You know how it is: you're twenty-one or twenty-two and you make some decisions; then whisssh! you're seventy: you've been a lawyer for fifty years, and that white-haired lady at your side has eaten over fifty thousand meals with you.

How do such things begin?

George and Emily are going to show you now the conversation they had when they first knew that . . . that . . . as the saying goes . . . they were meant for one another.

But before they do it I want you to try and remember what it was like to have been very young.

And particularly the days when you were first in love; when you were like a person sleepwalking, and you didn't quite see the street you were in, and didn't quite hear everything that was said to you.

You're just a little bit crazy. Will you remember that, please?

Now they'll be coming out of high school at three o'clock. George has just been elected President of the Junior Class, and as it's June, that means he'll be President of the Senior Class all next year. And Emily's just been elected Secretary and Treasurer.

I don't have to tell you how important that is.

He places a board across the backs of two chairs, which he takes from those at the Gibbs family's table. He brings two high stools from the wings and places them behind the board. Persons sitting on the stools will be facing the audience. This is the counter of Mr. Morgan's drugstore. The sounds of young people's voices are heard off left.

Yepp,—there they are coming down Main Street now.

EMILY, *carrying an armful of—imaginary—schoolbooks, comes along Main Street from the left.*

EMILY:

I can't, Louise. I've got to go home. Good-by. Oh, Ernestine! Ernestine! Can you come over tonight and do Latin? Isn't that Cicero the worst thing—! Tell your mother you *have* to. G'by. G'by, Helen. G'by, Fred.

GEORGE, *also carrying books, catches up with her.*

GEORGE:

Can I carry your books home for you, Emily?

EMILY:

Coolly.

Why . . . uh . . . Thank you. It isn't far.

She gives them to him.

GEORGE:

Excuse me a minute, Emily.—Say, Bob, if I'm a little late, start practice anyway. And give Herb some long high ones.

EMILY:

Good-by, Lizzy.

GEORGE:

Good-by, Lizzy.—I'm awfully glad you were elected, too, Emily.

EMILY:

Thank you.

They have been standing on Main Street, almost against the back wall. They take the first steps toward the audience when GEORGE *stops and says:*

GEORGE:

Emily, why are you mad at me?

EMILY:

I'm not mad at you.

GEORGE:

You've been treating me so funny lately.

EMILY:

Well, since you ask me, I might as well say it right out, George,—

She catches sight of a teacher passing.

Good-by, Miss Corcoran.

GEORGE:

Good-by, Miss Corcoran.—Wha—what is it?

EMILY:

Not scoldingly; finding it difficult to say.

I don't like the whole change that's come over you in the last year. I'm sorry if that hurts your feelings, but I've got to—tell the truth and shame the devil.

GEORGE:

A *change*?—Wha—what do you mean?

EMILY:

Well, up to a year ago I used to like you a lot. And I used to watch you as you did everything . . . because we'd been friends so long . . . and then you began spending all your time at *baseball* . . . and you never stopped to speak to anybody any more. Not even to your own family you didn't . . . and, George, it's a fact, you've got awful conceited and stuck-up, and all the girls say so. They may not say so to your face, but that's what they say about you behind your back, and it hurts me to hear them say it, but I've got to agree with them a little. I'm sorry if it hurts your feelings . . . but I can't be sorry I said it.

GEORGE:

I . . . I'm glad you said it, Emily. I never thought that such a thing was happening to me. I guess it's hard for a fella not to have faults creep into his character.

They take a step or two in silence, then stand still in misery.

EMILY:

I always expect a man to be perfect and I think he should be.

GEORGE:

Oh . . . I don't think it's possible to be perfect, Emily.

EMILY:

Well, my *father* is, and as far as I can see *your* father is. There's no reason on earth why you shouldn't be, too.

GEORGE:

Well, I feel it's the other way round. That men aren't naturally good; but girls are.

EMILY:

Well, you might as well know right now that I'm not perfect. It's not as easy for a girl to be perfect as a man, because we girls are more—more—nervous.—Now I'm sorry I said all that about you. I don't know what made me say it.

GEORGE:

Emily,—

EMILY:

Now I can see it's not the truth at all. And I suddenly feel that it isn't important, anyway.

GEORGE:

Emily . . . would you like an ice-cream soda, or something, before you go home?

EMILY:

Well, thank you . . . I would.

They advance toward the audience and make an abrupt right turn, opening the door of Morgan's drugstore. Under strong emotion, EMILY *keeps her face down.* GEORGE *speaks to some passers-by.*

GEORGE:

Hello, Stew,—how are you?—Good afternoon, Mrs. Slocum.

The STAGE MANAGER, *wearing spectacles and assuming the role of Mr. Morgan, enters abruptly from the right and stands between the audience and the counter of his soda fountain.*

STAGE MANAGER:

Hello, George. Hello, Emily.—What'll you have?—Why, Emily Webb,—what you been crying about?

GEORGE:

He gropes for an explanation.

She . . . she just got an awful scare, Mr. Morgan. She almost got run over by that hardware-store wagon. Everybody says that Tom Huckins drives like a crazy man.

STAGE MANAGER:

Drawing a drink of water.

Well, now! You take a drink of water, Emily. You look all shook up. I tell you, you've got to look both ways before you cross Main Street these days. Gets worse every year.—What'll you have?

EMILY:

I'll have a strawberry phosphate, thank you, Mr. Morgan.

GEORGE:

No, no, Emily. Have an ice-cream soda with me. Two straw-berry ice-cream sodas, Mr. Morgan.

STAGE MANAGER:
Working the faucets.

Two strawberry ice-cream sodas, yes sir. Yes, sir. There are a hundred and twenty-five horses in Grover's Corners this min-ute I'm talking to you. State Inspector was in here yesterday. And now they're bringing in these auto-mo-biles, the best thing to do is to just stay home. Why, I can remember when a dog could go to sleep all day in the middle of Main Street and nothing come along to disturb him.

He sets the imaginary glasses before them.

There they are. Enjoy 'em.

He sees a customer, right.

Yes, Mrs. Ellis. What can I do for you?

He goes out right.

EMILY:
They're so expensive.

GEORGE:
No, no,—don't you think of that. We're celebrating our elec-tion. And then do you know what else I'm celebrating?

EMILY:
N-no.

GEORGE:

I'm celebrating because I've got a friend who tells me all the things that ought to be told me.

EMILY:

George, *please* don't think of that. I don't know why I said it. It's not true. You're—

GEORGE:

No, Emily, you stick to it. I'm glad you spoke to me like you did. But you'll *see:* I'm going to change so quick—you bet I'm going to change. And, Emily, I want to ask you a favor.

EMILY:

What?

GEORGE:

Emily, if I go away to State Agriculture College next year, will you write me a letter once in a while?

EMILY:

I certainly will. I certainly will, George . . .

Pause. They start sipping the sodas through the straws.

It certainly seems like being away three years you'd get out of touch with things. Maybe letters from Grover's Corners wouldn't be so interesting after a while. Grover's Corners isn't a very important place when you think of all—New Hampshire; but I think it's a very nice town.

GEORGE:

The day wouldn't come when I wouldn't want to know everything that's happening here. I know *that's* true, Emily.

EMILY:

Well, I'll try to make my letters interesting.

Pause.

GEORGE:

Y'know. Emily, whenever I meet a farmer I ask him if he thinks it's important to go to Agriculture School to be a good farmer.

EMILY:

Why, George—

GEORGE:

Yeah, and some of them say that it's even a waste of time. You can get all those things, anyway, out of the pamphlets the government sends out. And Uncle Luke's getting old,—he's about ready for me to start in taking over his farm tomorrow, if I could.

EMILY:

My!

GEORGE:

And, like you say, being gone all that time . . . in other places and meeting other people . . . Gosh, if anything like that can happen I don't want to go away. I guess new people aren't any better than old ones. I'll bet they almost never are. Emily . . . I feel that you're as good a friend as I've got. I don't need to go and meet the people in other towns.

EMILY:

But, George, maybe it's very important for you to go and learn all that about—cattle judging and soils and those things. . . . Of course, I don't know.

GEORGE:

After a pause, very seriously.

Emily, I'm going to make up my mind right now. I won't go. I'll tell Pa about it tonight.

EMILY:

Why, George, I don't see why you have to decide right now. It's a whole year away.

GEORGE:

Emily, I'm glad you spoke to me about that . . . that fault in my character. What you said was right; but there was *one* thing wrong in it, and that was when you said that for a year I wasn't noticing people, and . . . you, for instance. Why, you say you were watching me when I did everything . . . I was doing the same about you all the time. Why, sure,—I always thought about you as one of the chief people I thought about. I always made sure where you were sitting on the bleachers, and who you were with, and for three days now I've been trying to walk home with you; but something's always got in the way. Yesterday I was standing over against the wall waiting for you, and you walked home with *Miss Corcoran.*

EMILY:

George! . . . Life's awful funny! How could I have known that? Why, I thought—

GEORGE:

Listen, Emily, I'm going to tell you why I'm not going to Agriculture School. I think that once you've found a person that you're very fond of . . . I mean a person who's fond of you, too, and likes you enough to be interested in your character . . . Well, I think that's just as important as college is, and even more so. That's what I think.

EMILY:

I think it's awfully important, too.

GEORGE:

Emily.

EMILY:

Y-yes, George.

GEORGE:

Emily, if I *do* improve and make a big change . . . would you be . . . I mean: *could* you be . . .

EMILY:

I . . . I am now; I always have been.

GEORGE:

Pause.

So I guess this is an important talk we've been having.

EMILY:

Yes . . . yes.

GEORGE:

Takes a deep breath and straightens his back.

Wait just a minute and I'll walk you home.

With mounting alarm he digs into his pockets for the money.

The STAGE MANAGER *enters, right.*

GEORGE, *deeply embarrassed, but direct, says to him:*

Mr. Morgan, I'll have to go home and get the money to pay you for this. It'll only take me a minute.

STAGE MANAGER:

Pretending to be affronted.

What's that? George Gibbs, do you mean to tell me—!

GEORGE:

Yes, but I had reasons, Mr. Morgan.—Look, here's my gold watch to keep until I come back with the money.

STAGE MANAGER:

That's all right. Keep your watch. I'll trust you.

GEORGE:

I'll be back in five minutes.

STAGE MANAGER:

I'll trust you ten years, George,—not a day over.—Got all over your shock, Emily?

EMILY:

Yes, thank you, Mr. Morgan. It was nothing.

GEORGE:

Taking up the books from the counter.

I'm ready.

They walk in grave silence across the stage and pass through the trellis at the Webbs' back door and disappear.

The STAGE MANAGER *watches them go out, then turns to the audience, removing his spectacles.*

STAGE MANAGER:

Well,—

He claps his hands as a signal.

Now we're ready to get on with the wedding.

He stands waiting while the set is prepared for the next scene.

STAGEHANDS *remove the chairs, tables and trellises from the Gibbs and Webb houses.*

They arrange the pews for the church in the center of the stage. The congregation will sit facing the back wall. The aisle of the church starts at the center of the back wall and comes toward the audience.

A small platform is placed against the back wall on which the STAGE MANAGER *will stand later, playing the minister.*

The image of a stained-glass window is cast from a lantern slide upon the back wall.

When all is ready the STAGE MANAGER *strolls to the center of the stage, down front, and, musingly, addresses the audience.*

There are a lot of things to be said about a wedding; there are a lot of thoughts that go on during a wedding.

We can't get them all into one wedding, naturally, and especially not into a wedding at Grover's Corners, where they're awfully plain and short.

In this wedding I play the minister. That gives me the right to say a few more things about it.

For a while now, the play gets pretty serious.

Y'see, some churches say that marriage is a sacrament. I don't quite know what that means, but I can guess. Like Mrs. Gibbs said a few minutes ago: People were made to live two-by-two.

This is a good wedding, but people are so put together that even at a good wedding there's a lot of confusion way down deep in people's minds and we thought that that ought to be in our play, too.

The real hero of this scene isn't on the stage at all, and you know who that is. It's like what one of those European fellas said: Every child born into the world is nature's attempt to make a perfect human being. Well, we've seen nature pushing and contriving for some time now. We all know that nature's interested in quantity; but I think she's interested in quality, too,—that's why I'm in the ministry.

And don't forget all the other witnesses at this wedding,— the ancestors. Millions of them. Most of them set out to live two-by-two, also. Millions of them.

Well, that's all my sermon. 'Twan't very long, anyway.

The organ starts playing Handel's "Largo."

The congregation streams into the church and sits in silence.

Church bells are heard.

MRS. GIBBS *sits in the front row, the first seat on the aisle, the right section; next to her are* REBECCA *and* DR. GIBBS.

Across the aisle MRS. WEBB, WALLY *and* MR. WEBB. *A small choir takes its place, facing the audience under the stained-glass window.*

MRS. WEBB, *on the way to her place, turns back and speaks to the audience.*

MRS. WEBB:

I don't know why on earth I should be crying. I suppose there's nothing to cry about. It came over me at breakfast this morning; there was Emily eating her breakfast as she's done for seventeen years and now she's going off to eat it in someone else's house. I suppose that's it.

And Emily! She suddenly said: I can't eat another mouthful, and she put her head down on the table and *she* cried.

She starts toward her seat in the church, but turns back and adds:

Oh, I've got to say it: you know, there's something down-right cruel about sending our girls out into marriage this way.

I hope some of her girl friends have told her a thing or two. It's cruel, I know, but I couldn't bring myself to say anything. I went into it blind as a bat myself.

In half-amused exasperation.

The whole world's wrong, that's what's the matter.

There they come.

She hurries to her place in the pew.

GEORGE *starts to come down the right aisle of the theatre, through the audience.*

Suddenly THREE MEMBERS *of his baseball team appear by the right proscenium pillar and start whistling and catcalling to him. They are dressed for the ball field.*

THE BASEBALL PLAYERS:
Eh, George, George! Hast—yaow! Look at him, fellas—he looks scared to death. Yaow! George, don't look so innocent, you old geezer. We know what you're thinking. Don't disgrace the team, big boy. Whoo-oo-oo.

STAGE MANAGER:
All right! All right! That'll do. That's enough of that.

Smiling, he pushes them off the stage. They lean back to shout a few more catcalls.

There used to be an awful lot of that kind of thing at weddings in the old days,—Rome, and later. We're more civilized now,—so they say.

*The choir starts singing "Love Divine, All Love Excelling—." *GEORGE* has reached the stage. He stares at the congregation a moment, then takes a few steps of withdrawal, toward the*

right proscenium pillar. His mother, from the front row,
seems to have felt his confusion. She leaves her seat and comes
down the aisle quickly to him.

MRS. GIBBS:

George! George! What's the matter?

GEORGE:

Ma, I don't want to grow old. Why's everybody pushing
me so?

MRS. GIBBS:

Why, George . . . you wanted it.

GEORGE:

No, Ma, listen to me—

MRS. GIBBS:

No, no, George,—you're a man now.

GEORGE:

Listen, Ma,—for the last time I ask you . . . All I want to do
is to be a fella—

MRS. GIBBS:

George! If anyone should hear you! Now stop. Why, I'm
ashamed of you!

GEORGE:

He comes to himself and looks over the scene.

What? Where's Emily?

MRS. GIBBS:

Relieved.

George! You gave me such a turn.

GEORGE:

Cheer up, Ma. I'm getting married.

MRS. GIBBS:

Let me catch my breath a minute.

GEORGE:

Comforting her.

Now, Ma, you save Thursday nights. Emily and I are coming over to dinner every Thursday night . . . you'll see. Ma, what are you crying for? Come on; we've got to get ready for this.

MRS. GIBBS, *mastering her emotion, fixes his tie and whispers to him.*

In the meantime, EMILY, *in white and wearing her wedding veil, has come through the audience and mounted onto the stage. She too draws back, frightened, when she sees the congregation in the church. The choir begins: "Blessed Be the Tie That Binds."*

EMILY:

I never felt so alone in my whole life. And George over there, looking so . . . ! I *hate* him. I wish I were dead. Papa! Papa!

MR. WEBB:

Leaves his seat in the pews and comes toward her anxiously.

Emily! Emily! Now don't get upset. . . .

EMILY:

But, Papa,—I don't want to get married. . . .

MR. WEBB:

Sh—sh—Emily. Everything's all right.

EMILY:

Why can't I stay for a while just as I am? Let's go away,—

MR. WEBB:

No, no, Emily. Now stop and think a minute.

EMILY:

Don't you remember that you used to say,—all the time you used to say—all the time: that I was *your* girl! There must be lots of places we can go to. I'll work for you. I could keep house.

MR. WEBB:

Sh . . . You mustn't think of such things. You're just nervous, Emily.

He turns and calls:

George! George! Will you come here a minute?

He leads her toward George.

Why you're marrying the best young fellow in the world. George is a fine fellow.

EMILY:

But Papa,—

MRS. GIBBS *returns unobtrusively to her seat.*

MR. WEBB *has one arm around his daughter. He places his hand on* GEORGE'S *shoulder.*

MR. WEBB:

I'm giving away my daughter, George. Do you think you can take care of her?

GEORGE:

Mr. Webb, I want to . . . I want to try. Emily, I'm going to do my best. I love you, Emily. I need you.

EMILY:

Well, if you love me, help me. All I want is someone to love me.

GEORGE:

I will, Emily. Emily, I'll try.

EMILY:

And I mean for *ever*. Do you hear? For ever and ever.

They fall into each other's arms.

The March from Lohengrin *is heard.*

The STAGE MANAGER, *as* CLERGYMAN, *stands on the box, up center.*

MR. WEBB:

Come, they're waiting for us. Now you know it'll be all right. Come, quick.

GEORGE *slips away and takes his place beside the* STAGE MANAGER-CLERGYMAN.

EMILY *proceeds up the aisle on her father's arm.*

STAGE MANAGER:

Do you, George, take this woman, Emily, to be your wedded wife, to have . . .

MRS. SOAMES *has been sitting in the last row of the congregation.*

She now turns to her neighbors and speaks in a shrill voice. Her chatter drowns out the rest of the clergyman's words.

MRS. SOAMES:

Perfectly lovely wedding! Loveliest wedding I ever saw. Oh, I do love a good wedding, don't you? Doesn't she make a lovely bride?

GEORGE:

I do.

STAGE MANAGER:

Do you, Emily, take this man, George, to be your wedded husband,—

Again his further words are covered by those of MRS. SOAMES.

MRS. SOAMES:

Don't know *when* I've seen such a lovely wedding. But I always cry. Don't know why it is, but I always cry. I just like to see young people happy, don't you? Oh, I think it's lovely.

The ring.

The kiss.

The stage is suddenly arrested into silent tableau.

The STAGE MANAGER, *his eyes on the distance, as though to himself:*

STAGE MANAGER:

I've married over two hundred couples in my day.

Do I believe in it?

I don't know.

M. . . . marries N. . . . millions of them.

The cottage, the go-cart, the Sunday-afternoon drives in the Ford, the first rheumatism, the grandchildren, the second rheumatism, the deathbed, the reading of the will,—

He now looks at the audience for the first time, with a warm smile that removes any sense of cynicism from the next line.

Once in a thousand times it's interesting.

—Well, let's have Mendelssohn's "Wedding March"!

The organ picks up the March.

The BRIDE *and* GROOM *come down the aisle, radiant, but trying to be very dignified.*

MRS. SOAMES:

Aren't they a lovely couple? Oh, I've never been to such a nice wedding. I'm sure they'll be happy. I always say: *happiness,* that's the great thing! The important thing is to be happy.

The BRIDE *and* GROOM *reach the steps leading into the audience. A bright light is thrown upon them. They descend into the auditorium and run up the aisle joyously.*

STAGE MANAGER:

That's all the Second Act, folks. Ten minutes' intermission.

CURTAIN

—⚬—

Act III

During the intermission the audience has seen the stagehands arranging the stage. On the right-hand side, a little right of the center, ten or twelve ordinary chairs have been placed in three openly spaced rows facing the audience.

    These are graves in the cemetery.

    Toward the end of the intermission the ACTORS *enter and take their places. The front row contains: toward the center of the stage, an empty chair; then* MRS. GIBBS; SIMON STIMSON.

    The second row contains, among others, MRS. SOAMES.

    The third row has WALLY WEBB.

    The dead do not turn their heads or their eyes to right or left, but they sit in a quiet without stiffness. When they speak their tone is matter-of-fact, without sentimentality and, above all, without lugubriousness.

    The STAGE MANAGER *takes his accustomed place and waits for the house lights to go down.*

STAGE MANAGER:

This time nine years have gone by, friends—summer, 1913.

Gradual changes in Grover's Corners. Horses are getting rarer.

Farmers coming into town in Fords.

Everybody locks their house doors now at night. Ain't been any burglars in town yet, but everybody's heard about 'em.

You'd be surprised, though—on the whole, things don't change much around here.

This is certainly an important part of Grover's Corners. It's on a hilltop—a windy hilltop—lots of sky, lots of clouds,—often lots of sun and moon and stars.

You come up here, on a fine afternoon and you can see range on range of hills—awful blue they are—up there by Lake Sunapee and Lake Winnipesaukee . . . and way up, if you've got a glass, you can see the White Mountains and Mt. Washington—where North Conway and Conway is. And, of course, our favorite mountain, Mt. Monadnock, 's right here—and all these towns that lie around it: Jaffrey, 'n East Jaffrey, 'n Peterborough, 'n Dublin; and

Then pointing down in the audience.

there, quite a ways down, is Grover's Corners.

Yes, beautiful spot up here. Mountain laurel and li-lacks. I often wonder why people like to be buried in Woodlawn and Brooklyn when they might pass the same time up here in New Hampshire.

Over there—

Pointing to stage left.

are the old stones,—1670, 1680. Strong-minded people that come a long way to be independent. Summer people walk around there laughing at the funny words on the tombstones . . . it don't do any harm. And genealogists come up from Boston—get paid by city people for looking up their ancestors. They want to make sure they're Daughters of the American Revolution and of the *Mayflower*. . . . Well, I guess that don't do any harm, either. Wherever you come near the human race, there's layers and layers of nonsense. . . .

Over there are some Civil War veterans. Iron flags on their graves . . . New Hampshire boys . . . had a notion that the Union ought to be kept together, though they'd never seen more than fifty miles of it themselves. All they knew was the name, friends—the United States of America. The United States of America. And they went and died about it.

This here is the new part of the cemetery. Here's your friend Mrs. Gibbs. 'N let me see—Here's Mr. Stimson, organist at the Congregational Church. And Mrs. Soames who enjoyed the wedding so—you remember? Oh, and a lot of others. And Editor Webb's boy, Wallace, whose appendix burst while he was on a Boy Scout trip to Crawford Notch.

Yes, an awful lot of sorrow has sort of quieted down up here.

People just wild with grief have brought their relatives up to this hill. We all know how it is . . . and then time . . . and sunny days . . . and rainy days . . . 'n snow . . . We're all glad they're in a beautiful place and we're coming up here ourselves when our fit's over.

Now there are some things we all know, but we don't take'm out and look at'm very often. We all know that *something* is eternal. And it ain't houses and it ain't names, and it ain't earth, and it ain't even the stars . . . everybody knows in their bones that *something* is eternal, and that something has to do with human beings. All the greatest people ever lived have been telling us that for five thousand years and yet you'd be surprised how people are always losing hold of it. There's something way down deep that's eternal about every human being.

Pause.

You know as well as I do that the dead don't stay interested in us living people for very long. Gradually, gradually, they lose hold of the earth . . . and the ambitions they had . . . and the pleasures they had . . . and the things they suffered . . . and the people they loved.

They get weaned away from earth—that's the way I put it,—weaned away.

And they stay here while the earth part of 'em burns away, burns out; and all that time they slowly get indifferent to what's goin' on in Grover's Corners.

They're waitin'. They're waitin' for something that they feel is comin'. Something important, and great. Aren't they waitin' for the eternal part in them to come out clear?

Some of the things they're going to say maybe'll hurt your feelings—but that's the way it is: mother 'n daughter . . . husband 'n wife . . . enemy 'n enemy . . . money 'n miser . . . all those terribly important things kind of grow pale around here. And what's left when memory's gone, and your identity, Mrs. Smith?

He looks at the audience a minute, then turns to the stage.

Well! There are some *living* people. There's Joe Stoddard, our undertaker, supervising a new-made grave. And here comes a Grover's Corners boy, that left town to go out West.

JOE STODDARD *has hovered about in the background.* SAM CRAIG *enters left, wiping his forehead from the exertion. He carries an umbrella and strolls front.*

SAM CRAIG:

Good afternoon, Joe Stoddard.

JOE STODDARD:

Good afternoon, good afternoon. Let me see now: do I know you?

SAM CRAIG:

I'm Sam Craig.

JOE STODDARD:

Gracious sakes' alive! Of all people! I should'a knowed you'd be back for the funeral. You've been away a long time, Sam.

SAM CRAIG:

Yes, I've been away over twelve years. I'm in business out in Buffalo now, Joe. But I was in the East when I got news of my cousin's death, so I thought I'd combine things a little and come and see the old home. You look well.

JOE STODDARD:

Yes, yes, can't complain. Very sad, our journey today, Samuel.

SAM CRAIG:

Yes.

JOE STODDARD:

Yes, yes. I always say I hate to supervise when a young person is taken. They'll be here in a few minutes now. I had to come here early today—my son's supervisin' at the home.

SAM CRAIG:
Reading stones.

Old Farmer McCarty, I used to do chores for him—after school. He had the lumbago.

JOE STODDARD:

Yes, we brought Farmer McCarty here a number of years ago now.

SAM CRAIG:

Staring at Mrs. Gibbs' knees.

Why, this is my Aunt Julia . . . I'd forgotten that she'd . . . of course, of course.

JOE STODDARD:

Yes, Doc Gibbs lost his wife two-three years ago . . . about this time. And today's another pretty bad blow for him, too.

MRS. GIBBS:

To Simon Stimson: in an even voice.

That's my sister Carey's boy, Sam . . . Sam Craig.

SIMON STIMSON:

I'm always uncomfortable when *they're* around.

MRS. GIBBS:

Simon.

SAM CRAIG:

Do they choose their own verses much, Joe?

JOE STODDARD:

No . . . not usual. Mostly the bereaved pick a verse.

SAM CRAIG:

Doesn't sound like Aunt Julia. There aren't many of those Hersey sisters left now. Let me see: where are . . . I wanted to look at my father's and mother's . . .

JOE STODDARD:

Over there with the Craigs . . . Avenue F.

SAM CRAIG:

Reading Simon Stimson's epitaph.

He was organist at church, wasn't he?—Hm, drank a lot, we used to say.

JOE STODDARD:

Nobody was supposed to know about it. He'd seen a peck of trouble.

Behind his hand.

Took his own life, y' know?

SAM CRAIG:

Oh, did he?

JOE STODDARD:

Hung himself in the attic. They tried to hush it up, but of course it got around. He chose his own epy-taph. You can see it there. It ain't a verse exactly.

SAM CRAIG:

Why, it's just some notes of music—what is it?

JOE STODDARD:

Oh, I wouldn't know. It was wrote up in the Boston papers at the time.

SAM CRAIG:

Joe, what did she die of?

JOE STODDARD:

Who?

SAM CRAIG:

My cousin.

JOE STODDARD:

Oh, didn't you know? Had some trouble bringing a baby into the world. 'Twas her second, though. There's a little boy 'bout four years old.

SAM CRAIG:

Opening his umbrella.

The grave's going to be over there?

JOE STODDARD:

Yes, there ain't much more room over here among the Gibbses, so they're opening up a whole new Gibbs section over by Avenue B. You'll excuse me now. I see they're comin'.

From left to center, at the back of the stage, comes a procession. FOUR MEN *carry a casket, invisible to us. All the rest are under umbrellas. One can vaguely see:* DR. GIBBS, GEORGE, *the* WEBBS, *etc. They gather about a grave in the back center of the stage, a little to the left of center.*

MRS. SOAMES:

Who is it, Julia?

MRS. GIBBS:

Without raising her eyes.

My daughter-in-law, Emily Webb.

MRS. SOAMES:

A little surprised, but no emotion.

Well, I declare! The road up here must have been awful muddy. What did she die of, Julia?

MRS. GIBBS:

In childbirth.

MRS. SOAMES:

Childbirth.

Almost with a laugh.

I'd forgotten all about that. My, wasn't life awful—

With a sigh.

and wonderful.

SIMON STIMSON:

With a sideways glance.

Wonderful, was it?

MRS. GIBBS:

Simon! Now, remember!

MRS. SOAMES:

I remember Emily's wedding. Wasn't it a lovely wedding! And I remember her reading the class poem at Graduation Exercises. Emily was one of the brightest girls ever graduated from High School. I've heard Principal Wilkins say so time after time. I called on them at their new farm, just before I died. Perfectly beautiful farm.

A WOMAN FROM AMONG THE DEAD:

It's on the same road we lived on.

A MAN AMONG THE DEAD:

Yepp, right smart farm.

They subside. The group by the grave starts singing "Blessed Be the Tie That Binds."

A WOMAN AMONG THE DEAD:

I always liked that hymn. I was hopin' they'd sing a hymn.

Pause. Suddenly EMILY *appears from among the umbrellas. She is wearing a white dress. Her hair is down her back and tied by a white ribbon like a little girl. She comes slowly, gazing wonderingly at the dead, a little dazed.*

She stops halfway and smiles faintly. After looking at the mourners for a moment, she walks slowly to the vacant chair beside Mrs. Gibbs and sits down.

EMILY:
To them all, quietly, smiling.

Hello.

MRS. SOAMES:
Hello, Emily.

A MAN AMONG THE DEAD:
Hello, M's Gibbs.

EMILY:
Warmly.

Hello, Mother Gibbs.

MRS. GIBBS:
Emily.

EMILY:
Hello.

With surprise.

It's raining.

Her eyes drift back to the funeral company.

MRS. GIBBS:
Yes . . . They'll be gone soon, dear. Just rest yourself.

EMILY:

It seems thousands and thousands of years since I . . . Papa remembered that that was my favorite hymn.

Oh, I wish I'd been here a long time. I don't like being new here.—How do you do, Mr. Stimson?

SIMON STIMSON:

How do you do, Emily.

EMILY *continues to look about her with a wondering smile; as though to shut out from her mind the thought of the funeral company she starts speaking to Mrs. Gibbs with a touch of nervousness.*

EMILY:

Mother Gibbs, George and I have made that farm into just the best place you ever saw. We thought of you all the time. We wanted to show you the new barn and a great long ce-ment drinking fountain for the stock. We bought that out of the money you left us.

MRS. GIBBS:

I did?

EMILY:

Don't you remember, Mother Gibbs—the legacy you left us? Why, it was over three hundred and fifty dollars.

MRS. GIBBS:

Yes, yes, Emily.

EMILY:

Well, there's a patent device on the drinking fountain so that it never overflows, Mother Gibbs, and it never sinks below a certain mark they have there. It's fine.

Her voice trails off and her eyes return to the funeral group.

It won't be the same to George without me, but it's a lovely farm.

Suddenly she looks directly at Mrs. Gibbs.

Live people don't understand, do they?

MRS. GIBBS:
No, dear—not very much.

EMILY:
They're sort of shut up in little boxes, aren't they? I feel as though I knew them last a thousand years ago . . . My boy is spending the day at Mrs. Carter's.

She sees MR. CARTER *among the dead.*

Oh, Mr. Carter, my little boy is spending the day at your house.

MR. CARTER:
Is he?

EMILY:
Yes, he loves it there.—Mother Gibbs, we have a Ford, too. Never gives any trouble. I don't drive, though. Mother Gibbs, when does this feeling go away?—Of being . . . one of *them*? How long does it . . . ?

MRS. GIBBS:
Sh! dear. Just wait and be patient.

EMILY:
With a sigh.

I know.—Look, they're finished. They're going.

MRS. GIBBS:
Sh—.

The umbrellas leave the stage. DR. GIBBS *has come over to his wife's grave and stands before it a moment.* EMILY *looks up at his face.* MRS. GIBBS *does not raise her eyes.*

EMILY:

Look! Father Gibbs is bringing some of my flowers to you. He looks just like George, doesn't he? Oh, Mother Gibbs, I never realized before how troubled and how . . . how in the dark live persons are. Look at him. I loved him so. From morning till night, that's all they are—troubled.

DR. GIBBS *goes off.*

THE DEAD:

Little cooler than it was.—Yes, that rain's cooled it off a little. Those northeast winds always do the same thing, don't they? If it isn't a rain, it's a three-day blow.—

A patient calm falls on the stage. The STAGE MANAGER *appears at his proscenium pillar, smoking.* EMILY *sits up abruptly with an idea.*

EMILY:

But, Mother Gibbs, one can go back; one can go back there again . . . into living. I feel it. I know it. Why just then for a moment I was thinking about . . . about the farm . . . and for a minute I *was* there, and my baby was on my lap as plain as day.

MRS. GIBBS:

Yes, of course you can.

EMILY:

I can go back there and live all those days over again . . . why not?

MRS. GIBBS:

All I can say is, Emily, don't.

EMILY:

She appeals urgently to the stage manager.

But it's true, isn't it? I can go and live . . . back there . . . again.

STAGE MANAGER:

Yes, some have tried—but they soon come back here.

MRS. GIBBS:

Don't do it, Emily.

MRS. SOAMES:

Emily, don't. It's not what you think it'd be.

EMILY:

But I won't live over a sad day. I'll choose a happy one—I'll choose the day I first knew that I loved George. Why should that be painful?

THEY *are silent. Her question turns to the stage manager.*

STAGE MANAGER:

You not only live it; but you watch yourself living it.

EMILY:

Yes?

STAGE MANAGER:

And as you watch it, you see the thing that they—down there—never know. You see the future. You know what's going to happen afterwards.

EMILY:

But is that—painful? Why?

MRS. GIBBS:

That's not the only reason why you shouldn't do it, Emily. When you've been here longer you'll see that our life here is to forget all that, and think only of what's ahead, and be ready for what's ahead. When you've been here longer you'll understand.

EMILY:

Softly.

But, Mother Gibbs, how can I *ever* forget that life? It's all I know. It's all I had.

MRS. SOAMES:

Oh, Emily. It isn't wise. Really, it isn't.

EMILY:

But it's a thing I must know for myself. I'll choose a happy day, anyway.

MRS. GIBBS:

No!—At least, choose an unimportant day. Choose the least important day in your life. It will be important enough.

EMILY:

To herself.

Then it can't be since I was married; or since the baby was born.

To the stage manager, eagerly.

I can choose a birthday at least, can't I?—I choose my twelfth birthday.

STAGE MANAGER:

All right. February 11th, 1899. A Tuesday.—Do you want any special time of day?

EMILY:

Oh, I want the whole day.

STAGE MANAGER:

We'll begin at dawn. You remember it had been snowing for several days; but it had stopped the night before, and they had begun clearing the roads. The sun's coming up.

EMILY:

With a cry; rising.

There's Main Street . . . why, that's Mr. Morgan's drugstore before he changed it! . . . And there's the livery stable.

The stage at no time in this act has been very dark; but now the left half of the stage gradually becomes very bright—the brightness of a crisp winter morning. EMILY *walks toward Main Street.*

STAGE MANAGER:

Yes, it's 1899. This is fourteen years ago.

EMILY:

Oh, that's the town I knew as a little girl. And, *look,* there's the old white fence that used to be around our house. Oh, I'd forgotten that! Oh, I love it so! Are they inside?

STAGE MANAGER:

Yes, your mother'll be coming downstairs in a minute to make breakfast.

EMILY:

Softly.

Will she?

STAGE MANAGER:

And you remember: your father had been away for several days; he came back on the early-morning train.

EMILY:

No . . . ?

STAGE MANAGER:

He'd been back to his college to make a speech—in western New York, at Clinton.

EMILY:

Look! There's Howie Newsome. There's our policeman. But he's *dead;* he *died.*

The voices of HOWIE NEWSOME, CONSTABLE WARREN *and* JOE CROWELL, JR., *are heard at the left of the stage.* EMILY *listens in delight.*

HOWIE NEWSOME:

Whoa, Bessie!—Bessie! 'Morning, Bill.

CONSTABLE WARREN:

Morning, Howie.

HOWIE NEWSOME:

You're up early.

CONSTABLE WARREN:

Been rescuin' a party; darn near froze to death, down by Polish Town thar. Got drunk and lay out in the snowdrifts. Thought he was in bed when I shook'm.

EMILY:

Why, there's Joe Crowell. . . .

JOE CROWELL:

Good morning, Mr. Warren. 'Morning, Howie.

MRS. WEBB *has appeared in her kitchen, but* EMILY *does not see her until she calls.*

MRS. WEBB:

Chil-*dren!* Wally! Emily! . . . Time to get up.

EMILY:

Mama, I'm here! Oh! how young Mama looks! I didn't know Mama was ever that young.

MRS. WEBB:

You can come and dress by the kitchen fire, if you like; but hurry.

HOWIE NEWSOME *has entered along Main Street and brings the milk to Mrs. Webb's door.*

Good morning, Mr. Newsome. Whhhh—it's cold.

HOWIE NEWSOME:

Ten below by my barn, Mrs. Webb.

MRS. WEBB:

Think of it! Keep yourself wrapped up.

She takes her bottles in, shuddering.

EMILY:

With an effort.

Mama, I can't find my blue hair ribbon anywhere.

MRS. WEBB:

Just open your eyes, dear, that's all. I laid it out for you special—on the dresser, there. If it were a snake it would bite you.

EMILY:

Yes, yes . . .

She puts her hand on her heart. MR. WEBB *comes along Main Street, where he meets* CONSTABLE WARREN. *Their movements and voices are increasingly lively in the sharp air.*

MR. WEBB:

Good morning, Bill.

CONSTABLE WARREN:

Good morning, Mr. Webb. You're up early.

MR. WEBB:

Yes, just been back to my old college in New York State. Been any trouble here?

CONSTABLE WARREN:

Well, I was called up this mornin' to rescue a Polish fella—darn near froze to death he was.

MR. WEBB:

We must get it in the paper.

CONSTABLE WARREN:

'Twan't much.

EMILY:

Whispers.

Papa.

MR. WEBB *shakes the snow off his feet and enters his house.* CONSTABLE WARREN *goes off, right.*

MR. WEBB:

Good morning, Mother.

MRS. WEBB:

How did it go, Charles?

MR. WEBB:

Oh, fine, I guess. I told'm a few things.—Everything all right here?

MRS. WEBB:

Yes—can't think of anything that's happened, special. Been right cold. Howie Newsome says it's ten below over to his barn.

MR. WEBB:

Yes, well, it's colder than that at Hamilton College. Students' ears are falling off. It ain't Christian.—Paper have any mistakes in it?

MRS. WEBB:

None that I noticed. Coffee's ready when you want it.

He starts upstairs.

Charles! Don't forget, it's Emily's birthday. Did you remember to get her something?

MR. WEBB:

Patting his pocket.

Yes, I've got something here.

Calling up the stairs.

Where's my girl? Where's my birthday girl?

He goes off left.

MRS. WEBB:

Don't interrupt her now, Charles. You can see her at breakfast. She's slow enough as it is. Hurry up, children! It's seven o'clock. Now, I don't want to call you again.

EMILY:

Softly, more in wonder than in grief.

I can't bear it. They're so young and beautiful. Why did they ever have to get old? Mama, I'm here. I'm grown up. I love you all, everything.—I can't look at everything hard enough.

She looks questioningly at the STAGE MANAGER, *saying or suggesting: "Can I go in?" He nods briefly. She crosses to the inner door to the kitchen, left of her mother, and as though entering the room, says, suggesting the voice of a girl of twelve:*

Good morning, Mama.

MRS. WEBB:
Crossing to embrace and kiss her; in her characteristic matter-of-fact manner.

Well, now, dear, a very happy birthday to my girl and many happy returns. There are some surprises waiting for you on the kitchen table.

EMILY:
Oh, Mama, you *shouldn't* have.

She throws an anguished glance at the stage manager.

I can't—I can't.

MRS. WEBB:
Facing the audience, over her stove.

But birthday or no birthday, I want you to eat your breakfast good and slow. I want you to grow up and be a good strong girl.

That in the blue paper is from your Aunt Carrie; and I reckon you can guess who brought the post-card album. I found it on the doorstep when I brought in the milk—George Gibbs . . . must have come over in the cold pretty early . . . right nice of him.

EMILY:
To herself.

Oh, George! I'd forgotten that. . . .

MRS. WEBB:

Chew that bacon good and slow. It'll help keep you warm on a cold day.

EMILY:

With mounting urgency.

Oh, Mama, just look at me one minute as though you really saw me. Mama, fourteen years have gone by. I'm dead. You're a grandmother, Mama. I married George Gibbs, Mama. Wally's dead, too. Mama, his appendix burst on a camping trip to North Conway. We felt just terrible about it—don't you remember? But, just for a moment now we're all together. Mama, just for a moment we're happy. *Let's look at one another.*

MRS. WEBB:

That in the yellow paper is something I found in the attic among your grandmother's things. You're old enough to wear it now, and I thought you'd like it.

EMILY:

And this is from you. Why, Mama, it's just lovely and it's just what I wanted. It's beautiful!

She flings her arms around her mother's neck. Her MOTHER *goes on with her cooking, but is pleased.*

MRS. WEBB:

Well, I hoped you'd like it. Hunted all over. Your Aunt Norah couldn't find one in Concord, so I had to send all the way to Boston.

Laughing.

Wally has something for you, too. He made it at manual-training class and he's very proud of it. Be sure you make a big fuss about it.—Your father has a surprise for you, too; don't know what it is myself. Sh—here he comes.

MR. WEBB:

Off stage.

Where's my girl? Where's my birthday girl?

EMILY:

In a loud voice to the stage manager.

I can't. I can't go on. It goes so fast. We don't have time to look at one another.

She breaks down sobbing.

The lights dim on the left half of the stage. MRS. WEBB *disappears.*

I didn't realize. So all that was going on and we never noticed. Take me back—up the hill—to my grave. But first: Wait! One more look.

Good-by, Good-by, world. Good-by, Grover's Corners . . . Mama and Papa. Good-by to clocks ticking . . . and Mama's sunflowers. And food and coffee. And new-ironed dresses and hot baths . . . and sleeping and waking up. Oh, earth, you're too wonderful for anybody to realize you.

She looks toward the stage manager and asks abruptly, through her tears:

Do any human beings ever realize life while they live it?— every, every minute?

STAGE MANAGER:

No.

Pause.

The saints and poets, maybe—they do some.

EMILY:

I'm ready to go back.

She returns to her chair beside Mrs. Gibbs.

Pause.

MRS. GIBBS:

Were you happy?

EMILY:

No . . . I should have listened to you. That's all human beings are! Just blind people.

MRS. GIBBS:

Look, it's clearing up. The stars are coming out.

EMILY:

Oh, Mr. Stimson, I should have listened to them.

SIMON STIMSON:

With mounting violence; bitingly.

Yes, now you know. Now you know! That's what it was to be alive. To move about in a cloud of ignorance; to go up and down trampling on the feelings of those . . . of those about you. To spend and waste time as though you had a million years. To be always at the mercy of one self-centered passion, or another. Now you know—that's the happy existence you wanted to go back to. Ignorance and blindness.

MRS. GIBBS:

Spiritedly.

Simon Stimson, that ain't the whole truth and you know it. Emily, look at that star. I forget its name.

A MAN AMONG THE DEAD:

My boy Joel was a sailor,—knew 'em all. He'd set on the porch evenings and tell 'em all by name. Yes, sir, wonderful!

ANOTHER MAN AMONG THE DEAD:

A star's mighty good company.

A WOMAN AMONG THE DEAD:

Yes. Yes, 'tis.

SIMON STIMSON:

Here's one of *them* coming.

THE DEAD:

That's funny. 'Tain't no time for one of them to be here.—
Goodness sakes.

EMILY:

Mother Gibbs, it's George.

MRS. GIBBS:

Sh, dear. Just rest yourself.

EMILY:

It's George.

GEORGE *enters from the left, and slowly comes toward them.*

A MAN FROM AMONG THE DEAD:

And my boy, Joel, who knew the stars—he used to say it took
millions of years for that speck o' light to git to the earth.
Don't seem like a body could believe it, but that's what he
used to say—millions of years.

GEORGE *sinks to his knees then falls full length at Emily's feet.*

A WOMAN AMONG THE DEAD:

Goodness! That ain't no way to behave!

MRS. SOAMES:

He ought to be home.

EMILY:

Mother Gibbs?

MRS. GIBBS:

Yes, Emily?

EMILY:

They don't understand, do they?

MRS. GIBBS:

No, dear. They don't understand.

The STAGE MANAGER *appears at the right, one hand on a dark curtain which he slowly draws across the scene.*

In the distance a clock is heard striking the hour very faintly.

STAGE MANAGER:

Most everybody's asleep in Grover's Corners. There are a few lights on: Shorty Hawkins, down at the depot, has just watched the Albany train go by. And at the livery stable somebody's setting up late and talking.—Yes, it's clearing up. There are the stars—doing their old, old crisscross journeys in the sky. Scholars haven't settled the matter yet, but they seem to think there are no living beings up there. Just chalk . . . or fire. Only this one is straining away, straining away all the time to make something of itself. The strain's so bad that every sixteen hours everybody lies down and gets a rest.

He winds his watch.

Hm. . . . Eleven o'clock in Grover's Corners.—You get a good rest, too. Good night.

THE END

A Nephew's Note

—ᴍ—

2020

For nearly a quarter of a century, I have represented Thornton Wilder as his literary executor. Over this span of time, it is a rare day that I do not find myself involved with some aspect of *Our Town*—production considerations, permissions requests, translation matters, theater talkbacks, Skype sessions with casts and school classes—and more. When Thornton Wilder's name is mentioned, the fable of growing up, falling in love, marrying and dying in Grover's Corners, New Hampshire, is usually the first thought that comes to mind. That's the way it typically plays out with an author's most famous work, and has pretty much been that way for *Our Town* since it opened on Broadway at Henry Miller's theater on West 43rd Street on February 4, 1938.

Like thousands of young would-be thespians, I got to know *Our Town* up close as a high school freshman when I performed on a temporary stage in a school gymnasium. I recall being as frightened as a puppy in 1955, when I played the role of Professor Willard while at the same time trying to avoid playing myself. I am confident that hundreds of young Professor Willards across this country felt just the way I did—as have thousands of others who have performed the role since, some as recently as yesterday. There are, on average, more than three hundred productions of *Our Town* in the United States and Canada every year, and several dozen more throughout the rest of the world. (Recent international productions include Sri Lanka, Russia, Lithuania, Australia, China, Germany, Greece, Japan, and Hungary.) At least once a day, somewhere, *Our Town* means our town, the place where we all live, love, and die.

What have I learned during my tenure as executor about a play my uncle described as "the life of a village against the life of the stars?" I have learned that people often do indeed tear up, and even weep when they see *Our Town*. "Take along plenty of handkerchiefs," Thornton Wilder warned a reporter in 1938 during its original Broadway run, adding, "Strong men cry when they see it." He was right. On many an evening I have seen hankies at work, heard sniffles, and seen real tears on the faces of strong women and (even) men.

Throughout much of the last century the play, especially among critical circles, was commonly viewed as a moving, but flimsy, sentimental, patriotic depiction of life in small-town America at the dawn of the twentieth century. In 1977 Martin Seymour-Smith, in *Who's Who in Twentieth Century Literature*, observed that *Our Town* was "good theatre" but "empty of real thought," presumably a play evoking emotion for the wrong reasons. Edward Albee saw the source of emotion another way: "I can't even think about parts of [*Our Town*] without wanting to cry," he said in an interview in the late 1990s. "Not because it is cute and touching and greeting card time, but because it is so tough and so sad. And I don't understand why it's played so cute all the time. I've never seen a more misunderstood play."

If I have learned anything over the past two decades, it is that *Our Town* has been more deeply understood, thanks in part to a rising generation of directors and actors who know the play to be the drama described by the late A. R. Gurney in 1998 as "a starkly powerful meditation on death and human existence." As a result, in production after production, theaters have found highly creative and dramatically fresh ways to costume and stage it. The raw times in which we live play their part, too. Theaters increasingly turn to *Our Town* seeking a way to celebrate and depict hard-won lessons about the preciousness of life and community in the wake of trauma. Take, for example, Joanne Woodward's decision to produce *Our Town*, starring Paul Newman, at Westport Country Playhouse in Connecticut, and later on Broadway, in response to the 9/11 attacks. And following the 2017 suicide bombing at Manchester Arena in the UK, the Manchester Royal Exchange Theatre mounted an enormously moving, successful production of *Our Town* dedicated to the memory of those who had died.

I maintain no list of favorite *Our Town* productions. But as a sampling of the variety of productions that I have seen and admired, I can offer these examples: the use of a powerfully evocative translucent wall placed between the dead and the living (Dallas Theatre Center); a backdrop that evoked no less powerfully the plain, even ugly rehearsal stage on which the play was originally mounted (Westport Country Playhouse); the second act performed in an historic church next door to the theater (Arden Theater); all types of staging with seats on two, three, or four sides, even on a huge stage open to the stars (Oregon Shakespeare Festival); bringing hundreds of theater patrons on stage over the course of the play's run, as part of a rotating cast of the dead in Act III (Long Wharf Theater); a cast composed of deaf and hearing actors (Pasadena Playhouse); and the first-ever multilingual production of the play, performed in English, Spanish, and Haitian Creole (Miami New Drama).

In the Addendum to the Foreword of this book, Donald Margulies mentions *Our Town*'s 2009 off-Broadway production at the Barrow Street Theatre, directed by David Cromer, who also initially played the Stage Manager.* The theater held 151 seats, arranged around a floor-level, three-sided thrust stage with two tables and several chairs as scenery, and the choir in a small balcony area. The arrangement made for an extraordinarily intimate relationship between play and audience, heightened by the actors who, in casual modern dress, often performed among the audience. Emily's return from the dead was staged as an animated tableau-like scene that played off memory, imagination, and the use of sensory stimulation. A typical evening at Barrow Street, where the production, which opened on February 17, 2009, and closed after 654 performances setting the record for the longest running *Our Town* in history, left audiences stumbling into the night asking themselves if this could possibly be the same *Our Town* they remembered seeing or performing in or hearing about once upon a time.

Yes, it is the same play. My generation brings to it what Thornton Wilder's great friend in this century, the late poet and librettist of the *Our Town Opera*, J. D. McClatchy (1945–2018) calls "scars on our hearts." Namely, what we know from having lived and loved for a good spell. But the marvelous genius of *Our Town* is that it offers every generation from around the world a variety of touchstones—moments of connection to days spent on this earth, no matter how long one has lived. On March 9, 1939, after the play's German language premiere in Zürich, Switzerland's celebrated Shauspielhaus, the arresting report below appeared in Weltwoche. These were among the first words ever published abroad— possibly even the first—about a play called *Eine Kleine Stadt*, an American drama set in a small town in New Hampshire "jenseits der Massachusetts-Linie."

> *Our Town* is the work of a true poet. Its relevance is indisputable. And its relevance is not political or ideological—much less extrinsic and applicable only to its artistic means of expression—but rather intellectual and spiritual. Just as a tuning fork can cause a string tuned to that same tone to vibrate, the thoughts and feelings expressed in this play respond to the prevailing mood of contemporary humanity in the most apt and exact manner. We feel ourselves at home in this strange and exciting mixture of skepticism and passion, of irony and sentimentality, of pessimism and great, sweeping thoughts, just as someone in 1839 felt at home in the Gothic halls and nocturnal crypts of Romantic theater.**

So ends a few brief observations on what I have learned in recent years about Thornton Wilder's most famous play—a dramatic event set against the stars that ponders in a loving way the human race under its "layers and layers of nonsense." In the words of contemporary critic Jeremy McCarter, Wilder's mission for actors and audiences is "to make a little better sense of the funny, scary, bewildering business of being alive."

And the show goes on . . .

—Tappan Wilder
October 2019

* In addition to David Cromer, Michael Shannon, Michael McKean, Scott Parkinson, Jason Butler Harner, and Stephen Kunken, Helen Hunt played the role of Stage Manager in this production.
** The quotation appears on the flap of the play's German language publication by Verlag Oprecht Zürich (1944). English translation courtesy of Lisa Harries Schumann.

Overview

Thornton Wilder, Pulitzer Prize–winning, internationally acclaimed novelist, entered the decade of the 1930s determined to achieve still another great distinction: playwright in full Broadway standing. He appeared to have achieved this dream on Friday evening, February 4, 1938 at Henry Miller's Theatre on Forty-Third Street, when Frank Craven, the admired character actor, played the part of the Stage Manager in the premiere of *Our Town,* directed and produced by the legendary Jed Harris. The play concluded with the language used in this production: "They're resting in Grover's Corners. Tomorrow's going to be another day. Good night to you, too. Good night. Get a good rest." After a short, stunned silence, broken by audible sniffles in the house, the audience offered an ovation.

The next day, the phone rang off the hook with good news at the author's home ninety miles away in Hamden, Connecticut. A particularly informative call came from Wilder's greatest actor friend, Ruth Gordon, then starring as Nora in Wilder's adaption/translation of Ibsen's *A Doll's House,* also playing on Broadway and also directed by Harris. (It is forgotten that Wilder had two shows running in New York City at the same time in 1938.) Wilder reported the highlights of Gordon's call (including tears in the eyes of a Hollywood mogul) to Dwight Dana, his attorney, confidant, and keeper of Wilder's exchequer during the Great Depression. This letter is the earliest written record of the playwright's reaction to a theatrical opening that would have a defining influence on his reputation and bank account ever after. "Dear Dwight," he began:

> Funny thing's happened.
>
> Ruth phoned down. It's already broken a house record.
>
> In spite of the mixed reviews when the box-office opened Saturday morning there were 26 people in line; the line continued all day, and the police had to close it for ten minutes so that the audience could get into the matinee; and that $6,500 was taken in on that day—the two performances and the advanced sale.
>
> Imagine that!
>
> Friday night both Sam Goldwyn and Bea Lillie were seen to be weeping. Honest! . . .
>
> Isn't it astonishing, and fun and exhausting?

Our Town did indeed receive mixed reviews. Negative comments focused on whether it was "dramatic" enough to be called a play or merely what Robert Benchley in *The New Yorker* saw as "so much ersatz." John Gassner in *One Act Play Magazine* dismissed the play as "devoid of developed situations" and thus much less than "a major dramatic experience," and George Jean Nathan later called it "a stunt." *Time* thought that Wilder's effective use of "Chinese methods gives ten times as much 'theatre' as conventional scenery could give," but nevertheless found the third act full of disappointing "mysticism and high-flown speculation." The *New*

Masses, the left-wing journal, whose editor, Michael Gold, had famously trashed Wilder's fiction earlier in the decade, tipped its hat slightly to the work while delivering a salvo: "It is an exasperating play, hideous in its basic idea and beautiful in its writing, acting and staging." ("Hideous" was the playwright's favorable treatment of middle-class, bourgeois values and lives.)

But where it mattered, in such papers as the *Herald-Tribune,* the *World-Telegram,* the *Brooklyn Daily Eagle,* and even in the tabloid *Sunday Mirror,* the play's staging, acting, directing, and themes evoked powerful adjectives and praise. It was "beautiful," "touching," "one of the great plays of our day," "magnificent." Robert Colman in the *Mirror* pulled out all stops, proclaiming it "worthy of an honored place in any anthology of the American drama," as soon it would be, starting in 1940. Brooks Atkinson in the *New York Times,* the first among equals in influence, wrote a review of poetic intensity, hailing Wilder and Harris for a play that "transmuted the simple events of human life into universal reverie," and that contained nothing less than "a fragment of the immortal truth."

By February 14, box-office sales having held up well enough to justify moving the play to its permanent home, the Morosco Theatre, Wilder felt comfortable enough to write to his friend Lady Sibyl Colefax in London: "Lord! I can't believe it myself. It's the hit of the town. Almost everybody's got some reservations against it (including myself) but everybody's discussing it and going to see it."

The drama that made even Sam Goldwyn cry appears as "M Marries N" in a list of ideas for plays penned July 2, 1935. This precise language—is it possibly the oldest in the play?—survives in the final version, at the end of Act II, when the Stage Manager, as minister, says: "M. . . . marries N. . . . millions of them." This "alphabet" marriage appears less than two weeks after Wilder encountered, at his brother's wedding in New Jersey, the custom of the groom not seeing his bride on the wedding day until they meet at the church. This fact, as well as other references in the play to Wilder family events, has always made *Our Town* an unusually personal (and tearful) experience for his family.

Thanks to records, we know that "M Marries N" evolved into "Our Village" in 1936, and into "Our Town" by 1937. Wilder was a writer who could not do serious work at his home in Connecticut. It is no surprise, therefore, that *Our Town*'s creative journey encompassed transatlantic streamers; writing tables in hotels and hideaways in such varied places as the Caribbean island of St. Lucia (October 1936) and the MacDowell Colony in Peterborough, New Hampshire (June 1937); and such addresses in Switzerland in the fall of 1937 as Zurich, St. Moritz, Sils-Maria, Sils-Baselgia, Ascona, and Rüschlikon. Of these, the Veltin Studio at the MacDowell Colony and especially a room in the Hotel Belvoir in lakeside Rüschlikon (a small village outside Zurich—eight francs a day, including breakfast and lunch) were key locations where scenes and acts were written, discarded, and revised. And rain or shine, there was one other central ingredient in a Wilder writing day—a long walk. Those taken in the Peterborough and Lake Sunapee areas of New Hampshire, starting in 1923, set the stage in his mind for *Our Town*. Shortly after the play opened, Wilder quantified his walks in an interview: "At a rough guess, one day's walk is productive of one fifteen-minute scene. Everything I've ever done has come into being that way and I don't think I could work out an entire play or novel at a desk now if I tried."

The following excerpts from Wilder's letters open helpful

windows on the author's progress during the key summer months of 1937. As they indicate, he was, in this period, working on several plays at once. (A reading below touches on the importance of Wilder's one-act plays of 1931 as the tool chest he used to construct *Our Town*, among them *The Happy Journey to Trenton and Camden* and *Pullman Car Hiawatha*.)

June 24 from the MacDowell Colony to Alexander Woollcott. My darts thrown at perfection are being feathered and pointed in many tranquil hours in these woods. Three of them are being assembled at once. None are ready to leave behind me when I sail. I always think of Our Village as yours. It is intended to give you pleasure. The Happy Journey [*to Trenton and Camden*] is no longer part of it. The last act in the cemetery will be prodigious. [*Our Town* is dedicated to Woollcott, the critic and broadcaster. He included *The Happy Journey* in the 1935 edition of his influential *Woollcott Reader*.]

September 4 from Zurich to his family. I've begun the Second Act of "Our Town." It'll be awful hard to combine all the things, general and particular, that one would wish to say about love and marriage,— combine them in one long flowing musical curve. . . . And back into the First Act go some preparatory speeches: Amy "Mama, am I . . . am I nice lookin'?" Mother "Oh, go-on-with-you. All my children got good features. I'd be ashamed if they hadn't." [Amy was an earlier name for Emily.]

September 6 to Sibyl Colefax from Zurich. A scene that must not be morbid though it plunges deep in the unconfessed structure of the mind. The bride seems never to have seen the groom before, is terrified, fears him, appeals to the audience for help, draws her father over to the proscenium pillar, and asks him to run away with her to the South Sea, to anywhere. He too is haunted; over her head tells the audience that no girl should be married, that there is no anxious state in the world crueler than that of a young wife . . . then passes his hand over his forehead and trembling, reassures his daughter and leads her back to the clergyman.

September 22 to family from Sils-Baselgia. Wonderful place.

The great ghost of Nietzsche. . . . Last night my play got such an influx of new ideas that now it's the most beautiful play you can imagine.

September 25 to Sibyl Colefax from Zurich. It's raining and the pantomime of the funeral goes on over in a far corner of the stage and there are <u>ten umbrellas up.</u>

Every act has hymn-singing in it—the choir practice, the wedding, the funeral. And when the city-dwelling Americans get those homely ur-American hymns going through them,—Just as the negro spirituals bathed and supported "Green pastures."

Yes, the last act has lots of cold iron and grasping-the-nettle in it, but Sils-Maria gave it an ultimate Affirming Ring.

October 1 to Sibyl Colefax from Rüschlikon. I'm behind schedule. I had hoped on October first to be able to jump to Play No #2.

But it doesn't matter: "Our Town's" First and Second Acts are all fair-copied and I think "set." And that difficult cactus-spined third is moving into place every day.

Lord! What I got myself in for. A theologico-metaphysico-transcription from the *Purgatorio* with panels of American rural genre-stuff.

Isn't it awful?

While they are waiting there to have the Earth slip from them, does Dante's vesperal angel make its appearance?

Can we see by the turning of their heads, by a *recuillement* that Something has come?

First of all: do I believe it?

October 28 to family from Rüschlikon. Jed [Harris] telephoned from London for 20 minutes the other night. He wants to know if "Our Town" would be a good play for the Xmas season in New York. Would it?!! And guess who might act the lanky tooth picking stage-manager? Sinclair Lewis! He's been plaguing Jed to let him act for a long time; and there's a part for his famous New England parlor-trick monologues. Don't tell anybody anything about it . . . [Lewis played the Stage Manager later in summer stock.]

November 24 to Amy Wertheimer from Paris. I was summoned by Jed Harris to Paris and read him "Our Town"—a New Hampshire village explored by the techniques of Chinese Drama and of <u>Pull-man Car Hiawatha</u>. He was very enthusiastic and hurried home to America to put it on for the Xmas season. . . . I follow soon for rehearsals.

Wilder did not, in fact, finish *Our Town* in Europe, and no walks are recorded in the last two places associated with the completion of the acting script. To assure that end and get publicity for it, Harris snatched Wilder off the dock when he arrived home on the Queen Mary and imprisoned him on Long Island. (To quote one headline: WILDER LOCKED UP TILL HE FINISHES THAT PLAY OF HIS.) The prison, a cottage on Long Island in the swanky Cold Spring Harbor area, came with amenities, including cook and butler and much chintz.

More Spartan was the spot where Wilder finally completed the acting script on December 19, only a few days before rehearsals began: the Columbia University Club on Forty-Third Street, three blocks from Broadway. Writing to Dwight Dana, he coupled this good news with a distressing report that he had not yet signed a play contract with Jed Harris, with whom he was "in such a mess of friendship-collaboration sentiment . . . and with a sense of sense of guilt about the unfinished condition of the play that I can't pull myself together to insist." But what of *Our Town*'s prospects? Wilder reported that Frank Craven (who had a contract) thought it "a possibility that the play will be a smashing success." This feeling built among the cast and the few people admitted to observe rehearsals (they predicted "big things"), although Wilder was almost immediately discouraged by some of Harris's stage directions, and worst of all, his "tasteless additions" to Wilder's script. These irritations soon grew into a violent quarrel that poisoned their relationship.

Our Town's route to Broadway wound through Princeton and Boston. The premiere was a single performance at the McCarter Theatre in Princeton, New Jersey, on January 22, 1938. The play drew a ferociously negative review in *Variety* ("it will probably go down as the season's most extravagant waste of fine talent"), but the audience and Wilder saw it differently. Wilder wrote to Dana:

> The performance at Princeton was an undoubted success. The large theatre was sold out with standees. Take was 1900 dollars; Audience swept by laughter often; astonishment; and lots of tears; long applause at the end by an audience that did not move from its seats.

Boston was in some ways a very different story. *Our Town* arrived there for a scheduled two-week run at the Wilbur Theater starting Tuesday, January 25. It is popularly believed that the Boston critics panned the play. In *Fanfare* (1957), the legendary stage publicist Richard Maney paints this standard story as only a New Yorker can: "[The play's] reception was so chilly and attendance so wretched that the two-week engagement was pared to one. The American Athens wanted no truck with a play without scenery. To Beacon Hill Brahmins, such an omission was as confusing as tackling a grapefruit without a spoon."

Business *was* terrible at the Wilbur in Boston in 1938, as it was in other theaters in that especially difficult Great Depression year. But the reviews were not all pans. Wilder described them as "cautious but not unfavorable." Critics saw much to like in the play, but they were perplexed and mystified by its avant-garde features, as this lead from an Associated Press story suggests: SPEECH-MAKING BY "CORPSES" UNUSUAL FEATURE. Mordaunt Hall of the *Boston Evening Transcript*, a prominent voice, found the play "curious," but noted that it was "roundly applauded by last night's gathering." A *New York Times* piece painted a similar picture—a "puzzled" audience but one that nevertheless at the end "applauded unashamedly a touching, delicately written, warmly acted play that bears a distant resemblance in its technique to Chinese or Greek methods translated into New England terms."

In Boston, *Our Town* drew perhaps the most extraordinary headline in its history. In what Wilder described as a "bomb dropped on the cast," the day before the Boston opening Harris's companion, the actress Rosamond Pinchot, committed suicide at her home outside New York. The tragedy was reported on page 1 in the *Boston Post* January 25:

LINK SUICIDE TO NEW SHOW HERE

Rosamond Pinchot Said to Have Been Brooding
Over Failure to Win Part in "Our Town"

Whatever the differences between the sizes of the houses, the Princeton and Boston productions shared one similarity—tears. Now disturbed about the audience's reaction to the play, Wilder wrote to Sibyl Colefax:

Audiences heavily papered. Laughed and cried. The wife of the Governor of Mass took it on her self to telephone the box-office that the last act was too sad. She was right. Such sobbing and nose-blowing you never heard. Matinee audience, mostly women, emerged red-eyed, swollen faced, and mascara-stained. I never meant that; and direction is responsible for much of it; Jed is now wildly trying to sweeten and water-down the text.

Shaken by Pinchot's death, the poor attendance, and critics who refused to leap with excitement, and losing significant money, Harris faced three options for a drama in which he had great faith: close it (which he prepared to do); withdraw it for further work and try it out in another city (an idea apparently entertained, however briefly, with New Haven in mind); or arrange an earlier-than-planned New York opening. Harris chose the last, threw the cast into four days of rehearsals, and opened the play temporarily at Henry Miller's Theatre on Friday, February 4. Said to have tipped the balance toward that option were the opinions of several influential figures who came from New York to see the play, among them the playwright Marc Connelly. He declared *Our Town* "magnificent," and ready for Broadway. Wilder, now suffering physical symptoms of distress from the tension of it all, wrote Sibyl Colefax as rehearsals began in New York: "Marc [Connelly] and other have sent the rumors around N.Y. that Friday night will be one exciting occasion. Jed is charging $5.50 top, which is insane."

As noted, the *Our Town* opening was an exciting occasion. The original Broadway production did not, however, break records. To keep the production going during the difficult hot summer months, Wilder accepted royalty cuts that reached 50 percent. Business improved somewhat when he played the part of the Stage Manager for two weeks in September. The job earned him respectable kudos in the press. He also enjoyed himself, although the experience left him "alternately exhausted and dizzy."

On November 19, slightly more than ten months into the run, Harris closed *Our Town* in New York after 336 performances and took it out on what was projected to be a lengthy national tour. Three months and twelve cities later, on February 11, 1939, the tour ended abruptly in Chicago. Thomas Coley, an original cast member, recalled the reason in a memoir: "Jed noticed that Frank Craven was earning more each week than he, the producer-director. He came out to persuade Mr. Craven to reduce his percentage of the gross. They argued. Jed lost. In a rage, he closed the play, thus cutting off the nose to spite his face, and, incidentally, the noses of forty-seven actors plus the crew."

Although *Our Town* had a less than record-breaking launch, its subsequent history, measured in amateur and stock productions, earned it the "smashing success" that Craven had predicted on the eve of rehearsals. And it all happened quite quickly.

The play's amateur and stock rights, for example, became available for the first time on April 19, 1939. By December 31, 1940, the play (handled by Samuel French) had been performed on amateur stages in no fewer than 658 communities. The figure represented every state of the Union save one (Rhode Island), as well as the District of Columbia, Hawaii, and four Canadian provinces. This laid the foundation for the *Our Town* rule of thumb ever since: It is performed at least once each night somewhere in this country. Behind these figures lies a large cast play that has marvelous parts for young people, is not expensive to mount, is glorious to teach, and treats life, death, and love in such an immediate fashion as to leave indelible and typically nostalgic impressions on generations of students.

Our Town was also a hit from the beginning with stock companies. Through May 1944 it had already been performed forty-three times, principally in the era's summer theaters in New England and the mid-Atlantic states. Five of these productions featured Wilder as the Stage Manager. Since World War II, the pattern has continued, now tied to the growth of American regional theaters in the postwar period. Between 1970 and 1999, for example, the play was performed ninety-one times in professional stock and regional theaters across the country, and it has already been performed another sixteen times so far in the new century. The Long Wharf Theatre in New Haven, Connecticut, Wilder's home city, mounted the play's fiftieth-anniversary production, starring Hal Holbrook. Another landmark production occurred in 1976, at the Williamstown Summer Festival, when Geraldine Fitzgerald bowed as the first woman to play the Stage Manager.

Marc Connelly, one of the saviors of the play when it stumbled in Boston, played the Stage Manager when *Our Town* had its first major New York revival in 1944, a production Jed Harris directed. There have been four revivals since, the last two being Lincoln Center's Tony Award–winning production starring Spalding Gray in 1988 and the Westport Country Playhouse's successful production starring Paul Newman in 2002. Both productions were subsequently showcased in national public television releases. These first-class and/or stock productions routinely provide the opportunity for audiences, critics, and artists to explore the play and its artistry in a fresh way. The findings can be revelatory—witness playwright Lanford Wilson writing about the fiftieth-anniversary production in 1987 in the *New York Times:* "And where the hell did [Wilder] get the reputation for being soft? Let's agree never to say that again. Let's not be blinded by the homey cute surface from the fact that *'Our Town'* is a deadly cynical and acidly accurate play." After September 11, many theaters also saw in it what Richard Hamburger at the Dallas Theater Center spoke of as a reassuring "sense of continuity and community."

Our Town has also been an international success story, beginning with the first productions in 1938 in the Scandinavian countries. Isabel Wilder's letter to her brother Amos in the Readings that follow opens a small window onto a large story, itself a reminder that the play's themes, so commonly identified as quintessentially American, have universal appeal. For example, since 1960, *Unsere kleine stadt* has been produced in at least twenty-two languages in twenty-seven countries, outside of Germany, and translated and almost certainly performed in more. (Precise figures can be hard to come by in this chapter of *Our Town*'s history.) Germany has always been a special case for this play as well as Wilder's other works. Between 1950 and 1970, *Our Town* was produced professionally eighty times in Germany; although it is done less often now, it continues to be performed and read in schools. It says much about the drama's planetary appeal and vision that the cover of the new German paperback edition depicts a major metropolis.

Despite many requests, Wilder did not permit *Our Town* to be fashioned into a live musical or opera. But he was open to other options. Forgotten is the play's extensive radio history, launched in March 1938 with a segment of *The Kate Smith Hour* (then the nation's most popular radio show) and including a six-month Camel Caravan series during World War II, and Wilder's own appearance in a *Theatre Guild on the Air* broadcast in September 1946. With one notable exception the play's early record in television (with Art Carney and Henry Fonda among headliners) is also forgotten. The exception is the ninety-minute musical Producer's Showcase version in 1955 starring Frank Sinatra, Paul Newman, and Eva-Marie Saint, remembered because of the continuing popularity of the award-winning Sammy Cahn–Jimmy Van Heusen song "Love and Marriage." In 1977, Hal Holbrook played the lead role in an admired two-hour NBC broadcast, a tradition of televising the "straight play" that the productions with Spalding Gray and Paul Newman have built upon since.

Thanks to cable television, movie cassettes, and DVD, the *Our Town* movie released by Sol Lesser at a huge celebration in Boston in May 1940 continues to have a public presence. (This time, *Our Town* was a success in that city.) Wilder, who had credentials as a screenwriter, was not initially interested in any participation in the script. But to protect his increasingly valuable property, he became deeply involved in it, including the famous decision to let Emily live (she dies only in a dream). He expressed his view on the matter this way in a letter to Lesser (thereby providing countless students with a term-paper subject):

> I've always thought [Emily should live]. In a movie you see the people so close to that a different relation is established. In the theatre they are halfway abstractions in an allegory; in the movie they are very concrete. So in so far as the play is a Generalized Allegory she dies—we die—they die; in so far as it's a Concrete Happening it's not important that she die. Let her live—the idea will have been imparted anyway.

As part of the record, it is important to add that it never occurred to Wilder that technology would give the *Our Town* film such a long afterlife, and that his permission for a one-time-only televised performance of the Cahn–Van Heusen musical would yield the song "Love and Marriage," still sung and hummed—and enjoyed—by millions.

He was glad to have the money that the rights for the two shows yielded, but then he found he had to live with the contribution they made throughout much of the twentieth century to a popular view of *Our Town* as a sentimental and nostalgic work of art.

A month after the Broadway opening Wilder had fled to Arizona to complete *The Merchant of Yonkers,* a second play that had made the earlier trip to Switzerland. It is clear from letters that he was thinking hard about what he had learned about playwriting from his *Our Town* experience. He credited Jed Harris for much of its success, and would approach him two more times to direct new plays. (Harris passed.) But it is also clear that he never believed Harris fully grasped the deeper meaning of his play. In March 1938, from Arizona, he wrote his sister an opinion he appears never to have changed. The immediate context was that Eleanor Roosevelt had written a day earlier in her column "My Day" that the play had "depressed her beyond words."

> I've now decided that on one plane *Our Town* is a very pessimistic piece. But on a higher plane it isn't. That's where Jed fell down. If you hang the planets and the years high up above the play, you can get the Reconciliation but if you don't it's crushing. Jed gypped me on "the cosmic overtones" just where [Max] Reinhardt would be best.

Less than a year later, Reinhardt, the great German director whom Wilder had idealized since boyhood, took *Merchant* to Broadway—and failed dismally. After the war, the play was reborn as *The Matchmaker* and set a Wilder Broadway record of 486 performances, 110 more than *Our Town.* To quote Wilder (and many others): "Theater is a funny business."

In the end, the "funny business" that Wilder sought to conquer after 1930 blessed him with great artistic and monetary success. Where *Our Town* is concerned, one can go further. Thornton Wilder had two sensational moments in his lifetime—one in fiction, *The Bridge of San Luis Rey,* and one in drama, *Our Town.* Had he been a baseball player, they could be compared to hitting grand slams in the bottom of the ninth with his team three runs down.

Sensations cast long shadows. *Our Town*'s shadow is especially long and deep. It is the grand slam at the last out of the last game of the World Series. It says much about the author's drive and his sense of himself that the play's success did not cripple his art; Wilder was incapable of resting on laurels. He went on to write more plays and novels, including another Pulitzer Prize–winning drama and a novel that received the National Book Award, and busied himself to the day of his death with such a host of other literary deeds that he earned among the cognoscenti the reputation as a man of letters rather than only a novelist or a playwright.

But the *Our Town* shadow was long and deep—and remains so. When Wilder's turn came in 1997 to end up on a stamp, the artist did not hesitate to depict him against the backdrop of a New England landscape. The sun is setting and soon the village will be set against "the life of the stars." That is where Thornton Wilder rests.

—Tappan Wilder
2003

Thornton Wilder stamp issued on April 17, 1997, in the Thornton Wilder Hall at the Miller Memorial Central Library in Hamden, Connecticut.

Readings

—∿—

Pre–*Our Town*

Our Town on the Boards

Special Features and Legacy

L'Envoi

Pre–*Our Town*

—⁓—

1. A Wedding:
Wilder Encounters a Superstition

Many of the moments of family life in *Our Town*—the table talk among the children, etc.—are drawn from Thornton Wilder's memories of his own upbringing. The famous line "Pretty enough for all normal purposes" was a family "classic," and the specific mention of North Conway recalls his older brother Amos's years there from 1925 to 1928 as minister of the First Congregational Church. On June 26, 1935, Wilder served as best man in his brother's wedding to Catharine Kerlin in Moorestown, New Jersey. It was here, in the Kerlin family home, that he witnessed the future mother-in-law inform the groom at breakfast on the wedding day that he would not see his bride until the ceremony. The wedding took place in the garden. Honoring the theatrical importance of this wedding, Catharine Kerlin Wilder's bridal dress is now on permanent display at the Historical Society of Moorestown.

Pictured left to right: Amos Niven Wilder, Catharine Kerlin, and
Thornton Niven Wilder

2. Life, Death, and Understanding in Wilder's Earlier Fiction and Drama

Fiction: "Once Upon a Time . . ."

Our Town, as the playwright often pointed out, was inspired in part by the story related by Chrysis the *hetaira* (courtesan) to the young men on the island of Byrnos in Wilder's best-selling novel of 1930, *The Woman of Andros*. Zeus seeks a favor that the King of the Dead cannot deny, much as he would like to. In the story, set in the pre-Christian era, we find an all but word-by-word foreshadowing of the scene when Emily returns from the dead in a no-less-mythical place on her twelfth birthday—and now understands. Fascinated by the power of memory and imagination in our lives, Wilder in 1930 described one of the themes of the novel in language echoed in Readings 3 and 6: "The difference between the matter-of-factness and almost the triviality of life as we live it and the emotion and beauty of the same life when we remember it, looking backward from years later."

Once upon a time there was a hero who had done a great service to Zeus. When he came to die and was wandering in the gray marshes of hell, he called to Zeus, reminding him of that service and asking a service in return: he asked to return to earth for one day. Zeus was greatly troubled and said that it was not in his power to grant this, since even he could not bring above ground the dead who had descended to his brother's kingdom. But Zeus was so moved by the memory of the past that he went to the palace of his brother and, clasping his knees, asked him to accord him this favor. And the King of the Dead was greatly troubled, saying that even he who was King of the Dead could not grant this thing without involving the return to life in some difficult and painful condition. But the hero gladly accepted whatever difficult or painful condition was involved, and the King of the Dead permitted him to return not only to the earth, but to the past, and to live over again that day in all the twenty-two thousand days of his lifetime that had been least eventful, but it had to be with a mind divided into two persons: the participant who does the deeds and says the words of so many years before, and the onlooker who foresees the end. So the hero returned to the sunlight and to a certain day in his fifteenth year . . .

As he awoke in his boyhood's room, pain filled his heart—not only because it had started beating again, but because he saw the walls of his home and knew that in a moment he would see his parents, who lay long since in the earth of that country. He descended into the courtyard. His mother lifted her eyes from the loom and greeted him and went on with her work. His father passed through the court unseeing, for on that day his mind had been full of care. Suddenly the hero saw that the living too are dead and that we can only be said to be alive in those moments when our hearts are conscious of our treasure; for our hearts are not strong enough to love every moment. And not an hour had gone by before the hero, who was both watching life and living it, called on Zeus to release him from so terrible a dream. The gods heard him, but before he left he fell upon the ground and kissed the soil of the world that is too dear to be realized.

Drama: "Good-By, Emerson Grammar School"

Our Town is also the dramatic child of the three experimental one-act plays that Thornton Wilder published in 1931, *The Long Christmas Dinner, The Happy Journey to Trenton and Camden,* and *Pullman Car Hiawatha.* In them, he employed such methods as minimal scenery, time compression, pantomime, and a stage manager as actor in one or in multiple parts, as he would do later in *Our Town.* The one-acts also explore Wilder themes already well established in his fiction, among them the repetition of family life. *Chicago Tribune* critic Fanny Butcher in 1931 described *Pullman Car Hiawatha* as "the chorus of life and death and man's relation to time and space." Managed by Samuel French after 1932, Wilder's one-acts had been produced widely by amateur groups by the time of the *Our Town* opening, thus helping to seed interest in his first full-length play when it first became available for amateur productions in April 1939.

The following scene is from *Pullman Car Hiawatha.* Harriet, married to Philip, dies as the train makes its way from New York to Chicago (passing through Grover's Corners, Ohio, along the way). The angel Gabriel and two archangels usher her to her death by climbing steps at the end of a train car, which is staged with chairs. This brief excerpt includes her last words, in form and cadence and actual words not unlike Emily's in *Our Town.* Wilder attended the Emerson Grammar School in Berkeley, California. He took great pleasure in using his play to thank several of his schoolteachers.

HARRIET:
Oh, I'm ashamed! I'm just a stupid and you know it.
I'm just another American. But then what wonderful

things must be beginning now. You really want me? You really want me?

They [THE ARCHANGELS] *start leading her down the aisle of the car.*

Let's take the whole train. There are some lovely faces on this train. Can't we all come? You'll never find anyone better than Philip. Please, please, let's all go.

They reach the steps. THE ARCHANGELS *interlock their arms as a support for her as she leans heavily on them, taking the steps slowly. Her words are half singing and half babbling.*

But look at how tremendously high and far it is. I've a weak heart. I'm not supposed to climb stairs. "I do not ask to see the distant scene: one step enough for me." It's like Switzerland. My tongue keeps saying things. I can't control it. Do let me stop a minute: I want to say good-by.

She turns in their arms.

Just a minute, I want to cry on your shoulder.

She leans her forehead against GABRIEL's *shoulder and laughs long and softly.*

Good-by, Philip. I begged him not to marry me, but he would. He believed in me just as you do. Good-by 1312 Ridgewood Avenue, Oaksbury, Illinois. I hope I remember all its steps and doors and wallpapers forever. Good-by, Emerson Grammar School on the corner of Forbush Avenue and Wherry Street. Good-by, Miss Walker and Miss Cramer who taught me English and Miss Matthewson who taught me biology. Good-by, First Congregational Church on the corner of Meyerson Avenue and Sixth Street and Dr. McReady and Mrs. McReady and Julia. Good-by, Papa and Mama . . .

She turns.

Now I'm tired of saying good-by. I never used to talk like this. I was so homely I never used to have the courage to talk. Until Philip came. I see now. I see now. I understand everything now.

Photo by Richard Anderson Productions

Pullman Car Hiawatha at Centerstage Theater in Baltimore in 2001 with Angela Reed as Harriet, and Craig Mathers and Willy Conley as archangels

3. *Our Town* in the Making: Four Drafts

——〜——

What follows suggests something of the script at various stages of development. The trend is always toward an ever more spare and direct style and focus on Grover's Corners.

"M Marries N": The Birth of the Play (1935)

The stage manager uses chalk to draw the outline of the railroad car in *Pullman Car Hiawatha*. This technique is also used in this excerpt from *Our Town*'s earliest known progenitor, a twelve-page sketch titled "M Marries N," written soon after Wilder's brother Amos's wedding in June 1935. Its focus is a young couple, George and Anne, discovering they are in love, and concludes with these lines:

GEORGE:
You do like me, too, don't you, Anne?

ANNE:
Y-e-s.

GEORGE:
Anne, I guess I more than like you.

> *They stand a moment in silence—looking at the ground.*

In the scene, set after a school day, he is carrying her books. It includes many features found in *Our Town,* among them a soda fountain and a trellis. Grover's Corners, New Hampshire, still lies in the future. "M Marries N" is set in "an American village," also identified in the text as "Hamilton in such-and-such a State." In addition to a stage manager, the cast includes a seated fisherman, described later as "Old Philosopher, Old Irony himself, Old gimlet-eye," a figure inspired by Chinese drama.

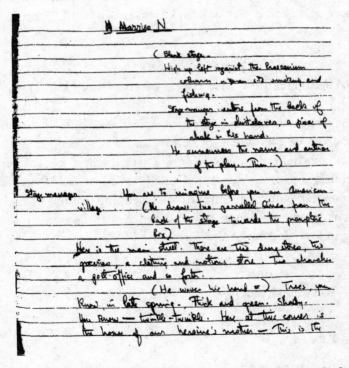

The first page of "M Marries N," Thornton's earliest known draft of what would become *Our Town*

Transcription of page from "M Marries N" and subsequent half page:

> *Blank stage—High up left against the Proscenium column, a man sits smoking and fishing—Stage manager enters from the back of the stage in shirt-sleeves, a piece of chalk in his hand. He announces the name and author of the play. Then:*

STAGE MANAGER:

You are to imagine before you an American village.

> *He draws two parallel lines from the back of the stage towards the prompter's box.*

Here is the main street. There are two drug stores, two groceries, and a clothing and notions store. Two churches, a post office and so forth.

> *He waves his hand.*

Trees; you know, in late spring. Thick and green. Shady. You know—twinkle-twinkle. Here at this corner is the home of our heroine's mother—This is the back door—

> *Two assistants push out a trellis covered with morning glories and a revolving "tree" for drying laundry on—*

On this side is the favorite drug store. Here's the counter.

> *Two assistants go to the left and push out a counter. A rack of onyx-knobbed faucets—strawberry flavoring, chocolate flavoring and so on. They put four high stools before it.*

Grover's Corners, New Hampshire, "Latitude 71° 37´, Longitude 42° 40´" (1937)

Reproduction of page ₁o f the 1937 ᵈ raft of *Our Town*

The image above is exhibited in Wilder's Yale College twentieth-reunion class book (1940). It is captioned, "Reproduction of Page One of the Original Manuscript of *Our Town*." Notable features include the use still of chalk by the Stage Manager (as in *Pullman Car Hiawatha*), the playful interaction with the audience from the start, and two brief commedia dell'arte–like entertainments for intermissions. *The Long Christmas Dinner* traces a family through ninety years, the inspiration for the original scheme for Act II of *Our Town,* a one-hundred-year history of the Webb family. The latitude and longitude lines are changed in the final version. Neither identifies New Hampshire. (The coordinates shown here mark southern Greenland. Grover's Corners in its final version is located in deep water about a thousand feet off Wharf Road in Rockport, Massachusetts.)

Transcription of page 1 of the 1937 draft of *Our Town*:

OUR TOWN
(Act II missing) play in Three Acts.
(No curtain.
(No scenery.
When the house-lights go down, the STAGE MANAGER *in overalls, has been leaning up for some time against the proscenium pillar, smoking a cigarette, and staring drily at the arrivals in the audience. At last, in a very Yankee accent, he begins to speak:*

STAGE MANAGER:
This play is called "*Our Town*." It was written by Thornton Wilder. It is produced and directed by Jed Harris, and it is acted by Miss X, Miss Y, Miss Z; Mr. A, Mr. B., Mr. C; and many others.

The First Act shows a day in *Our Town*; the second act shows a century in our first family's home, and the last act shows—well, you'll see.

Between the First Act and the Second, there will be played an interlude called "The Pleasures and Penalties of Automobiling"; and between the Second and Third Acts, there will be another interlude—a propaganda piece called "Is the Devil Entitled to a Vote?"

Are you ready?

He looks at the lady who arrived late. She shakes her head amused, saying Tz-Tz-Tz, implying What'll they do next!

This is *Our Town*, Grover's Corners, New Hampshire. It's near the Massachusetts line—Latitude 71° 37′, Longitude, 42° 40′. The date is Friday, May 7, 1907.

He looks hard at the lady again and repeats "1907."

It's dawn.

The sky is beginning to show some streaks of light behind our mountain, over in the East there. The morning star is doing that last excitement it always goes into just before dawn.

I'll draw the plan of the town for you.

Chalk in hand he goes to the back of the stage and draws two parallel lines down the center of the stage toward the footlights.

Way back here is the railroad station and the . . .

"Good Night to You All, and Thank You" (1937)

This version of the play's closing lines, worked on in Switzerland and subsequently revised, includes a ghostlike evening "visit." In final form, Emily inherits Mrs. Gibb's lines about understanding, and George "sinks to his knees then falls full length at Emily's feet" rather than flinging himself down, as he does here. A transcript of this text follows.

Final page of the 1937 draft of *Our Town*

Transcription:

> *The chairs are being replaced for the cemetery. The "dead" come on, and gather about her.*

EMILY:

I didn't listen to you. Now I just want to be quiet for a while. That's all human beings are—just blind people.

MRS. GIBBS:

Sh! Sh! It's evening now. The Evening Visit.

EMILY:

What visit?

MRS. GIBBS:

Sh.

Apparently something has appeared to them, invisible to us. They all face it, with breathless attention, and follow it as it crosses the stage, like a breeze across a wheatfield, each bows his head slightly in succession. When it has gone EMILY *whispers enthralled:*

EMILY:

Every evening?

MRS. GIBBS:

And morning?

EMILY:

The weight's gone. . . . Let me sit by you.

She leans her head against MRS. GIBBS *[sic] shoulder.*

GEORGE *enters. He comes and stands a moment before his mother's chair, his lower lip pressed hard against his upper. Then he goes over to the corner where Emily's grave is. He stands a moment; then flings himself full length upon the stage.* EMILY *raises her head and stares into her mother's face.*

MRS. GIBBS *(softly):*

They don't believe what they're told. They don't listen to what they're [sic] heart tells them, do they?

STAGE MANAGER
(back at his proscenium with a cigarette):

That's all there is of this play. Good night to you all, and thank you.

"I'll run for something . . .": George Gibbs's Political Aspirations (1938)

GEORGE

(WITH BAIRD LOOK AT HER)

No, Emily, you stick to it. I'm glad you spoke to ..e like you
did. But you'll see: I'm going to change so quick - you bet
(SHE SIPS)
I'm going to change ᴧ And Emily, I want to ask you a favor.

EMILY

Wh--a--t?

GEORGE   *(The thought hurts
Emily and she turns DF*
Emily, if I go away to State Agriculture College next yearᴧ will
you write me a letter once in a while?

EMILY
(WINKS BACK TEARS)
I certainly will. I certainly will, George....
(SIPS)
(Pause)

It certainly seems like being away three years you'd get out of
touch with things.

GEORGE

No, no. I mustn't do that. You see, I'm not only going to be
just a farmer. After a while maybe I'll run for something to
get elected. So your letters'll be very important to me - you
know, telling me what's going on here and all.

EMILY

Just the same, three years is a long time. Maybe letters from
Grover's Corners wouldn't be so interesting after a while.
Grover's Corners isn't a very important place when you think of
all New Hampshire; but I think it's a very nice town.
(SIPS)
GEORGE

The day wouldn't come when I wouldn't want to know everything
about our town. I know that's true, Emily.

EMILY

Well, I'll try to make the letters interesting.

From the Stage Manager's prompt script, Act II of *Our Town*

This page is from the soda fountain scene from the *Our Town* production stage manager's "Prompt Script," the official record of the actual production. Assuming that George may leave Grover's Corners, we learn here that he harbors political ambitions and, in addition to merely corresponding with a good friend, may someday welcome local intelligence from a reliable source.

Are we surprised? There are always high school senior-class presidents who dream of becoming governors or even presidents, and adoring girlfriends who share their dreams. But Wilder's goal was immersion in a New Hampshire village that was "an allegorical representation of all life" (see Reading 6). In rehearsals a change was made—the key lines were deleted, as shown in this reading and as printed below. But a line related to the statewide scenario slipped into the wedding scene in the *Our Town* Samuel French Acting Edition where the Stage Manager says: "Maybe [Nature's] tryin' to make another good Governor for New Hampshire. That's what Emily hopes . . ." Wilder removed this line when he crafted his definitive version of *Our Town* in 1957.

Transcription:

EMILY:

It certainly seems like being away three years you'd get out of touch with things.

GEORGE:

No. No. I mustn't do that. You see, I'm not only going to be just a farmer. After a while maybe I'll run for something to get elected. So your letters'll be very important to me—you know, telling me what's going on here and all.

[with a pick up in Emily's speech] ". . . Maybe letters from Grover's Corners . . ." etc.

4. The Writing of *Our Town*: Here and Abroad

MacDowell colonists—artists, writers, musicians, and architects—work in solitude, each in a separate studio, on a four-hundred-acre farm of woodland and meadow in Peterborough, New Hampshire. Wilder made nine official visits to MacDowell between 1924 and 1953. During his sixth, in June 1937, he worked almost exclusively on *Our Town* in Veltin Studio, shown here.

Veltin Studio, the MacDowell Colony in Peterborough, New Hampshire

His walks through the countryside and the town were important influences on the work. Local legend has it that Fletcher Dole and Albert E. Campbell, respectively Peterborough's milkman and druggist in this period, inspired the characters in the play. (Both were members of a delegation, led by the governor, that attended the world premiere of the *Our Town* film in Boston in May 1940.) When asked if he knew Wilder, Dole is reputed to have replied, "Nope, but he knew me." When asked if Peterborough was *Our Town*, Wilder always shifted the question to a global perspective, as in this reply to reporter John Stevens, who was in Peterborough to cover Wilder receiving the first Edward MacDowell Medal in the summer of 1960:

> "Young man," he said, "Grover's Corners is your home town in New York and mine in Wisconsin. It's everyone's home town. I have received letters from people in Chile, Iran and Iraq who have read or seen the play. Despite sociological differences, they tell me they have readily identified their everyday experiences with those of *Our Town*'s George Briggs [sic] and Emily Webb, and Howie Newsome and the tormented, dipsomaniacal Beethoven trapped in Grover's Corners . . ." (*New York Times*, August 21)

The revisions of the first two acts and much work on the final version of Act III of *Our Town* occurred in Switzerland, where Wilder spent two months in September 1937. He was based at the Hotel Belvoir in Rüschlikon on the edge of Lake Zurich some five miles from the center of Zurich. Here he combined his writing with long walks along the lake and into the city and brief side trips out of town. Because of the importance of *Our Town*, the Hotel Belvoir can be described as one of the most famous addresses in Wilder's peripatetic life as a creative artist.

He had already published novels set in such exotic places

The Hotel Belvoir in Rüschlikon as it appeared in the 1930s

as seventeenth-century Peru and a mythical Greek island about two hundred years before the birth of Christ. He wrote in the late 1920s that his work was "French in form and manners (Saint-Simon and La Bruyère); German in feeling (Bach and Beethoven); and American in eagerness." By the middle and late 1930s the "eagerness" was evident in such short plays as *Pullman Car Hiawatha* and *The Happy Journey to Trenton and Camden* (both 1931), and in the novel *Heaven's My Destination* (1935). *Our Town* had expanded to evoke his signature, lifelong commitment to celebrating the connection between the commonplace and the cosmic dimensions of the lives of hardworking, humble, middle-class American men and women. (See next Reading.)

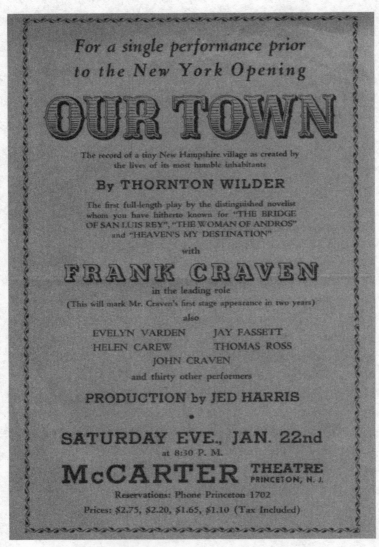

The *Princeton Flyer*—first advertisement for *Our Town*

Our Town on the Boards

—m—

5. In Production: Sample Images

The McCarter Theatre, Princeton, New Jersey (1938)

Our Town's first public performance took place at the the McCarter on January 22, 1938. The fine print of this advertisement reads, "The record of a tiny New Hampshire village as created by the lives of its most humble inhabitants." The premiere performance attracted an appreciative capacity audience. Wilder described it as composed of "fashionable villa colony; academic bourgeoisie; and students."

The Broadway Program (1938–39)

The following image is the cover of the program used during the play's run at the Morosco Theatre on Broadway. The dramatically large plume of smoke is a deadly accurate reminder of a defining feature of New Hampshire mill towns in the nineteenth and early twentieth centuries. Wilder was well aware of this satanic feature of these communities, offering glimpses of it in references to the successful Cartwright interests in manufacturing and banking. He would refer those interested in more details to Herman Melville's brutal short story "The Tartarus of Maids" (1855).

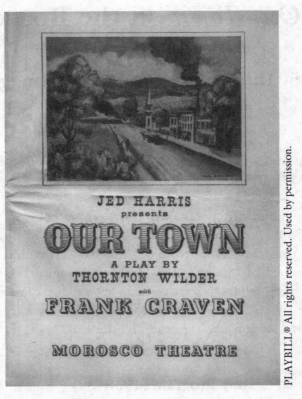

Our Town's first Broadway program

Two Original Cast Photographs

Photo by Vandamm, courtesy of the Billy Rose Collection, New York Public Library for the Performing Arts

Frank Craven (Stage Manager) and Arthur Allen (Professor Willard) in the original Broadway production of *Our Town* (1938)

This rarely reproduced Vandamm shot shows the Stage Manager (Frank Craven) instructing Professor Willard (Arthur Allen) in Act I "to sketch in a few details of our past history here." From the Boston preview, Wilder wrote Alexander Woollcott that Craven was "lovable" but had so much Irish blood that he left Wilder longing for "that deep, New England stoic irony that's grasped the iron of life and shares it with the house." He was likewise critical of Allen playing the part for laughs. "The Professor, adored by the audience

Photo by Vandamm, courtesy of the Billy Rose Collection, New York Public Library for the Performing Arts

Act III. Emily arrives at her grave for the first time.

and always clapped to the echo, is a caricature," Wilder wrote Woollcott. (The problem persists; it is always tempting to play this part for laughs.)

Because it gives a full sense of Wilder and Harris's use of the bare stage and depicts Emily's arrival at her grave in Act III, this Vandamm photo is the most widely reproduced shot of the original Broadway production. For many years it was included at the beginning of the acting edition. Martha Scott, who played Emily, was a last-minute addition to the cast. Wilder adored her performance.

The use of the bare stage was novel, but not unique, in 1938. *Life* magazine's extensive photographic coverage of the play was captioned "Thornton Wilder's '*Our Town*' is the latest in the Bare Stage." In addition to discussing other plays, the article included a reproduction of a *New Yorker* cartoon of the day showing three determined matinee ladies at a ticket booth. The first asks, "Does this play have scenery?"

6. The Playwright Discusses His Play

In company with most writers, Thornton Wilder did not believe it his job to both write and explain his novels and plays. Even so, he was always an enthusiastic champion for his work and put on quite a show when interviewed, as revealed here. The first is an interview given before *Our Town* had gone into rehearsals; the second is a preface to *Our Town,* published eight days after the Broadway opening; and last, an interview given four months later.

December 7, 1937—Before Rehearsals

"Sense of the Whole"

Our Town's producer-director Jed Harris let Wilder out of "prison" on Long Island to be interviewed for an article published on December 7, 1937, in the *New York World-Telegram,* from which this excerpt is taken. Wilder's words characteristically range over his calling, the nature and appeal of drama as an art form for the times, and the nature of his own play. *A Doll's House* opened in New York on January 27, 1938 and set a Broadway record for the work (144 performances). To write drama full-time, Wilder had given up his teaching post at the University of Chicago in 1936.

Jed Harris (Yale '21) has Thornton Wilder (Yale '20) under lock and key out Port Washington way. This is because Professor Wilder has to finish an original play called *Our Town* which Mr. Harris is waiting to put into rehearsal.

Every other day or so, however, Mr. Harris lets Mr. Wilder come to town (under surveillance); and in town he was today, pacing about Mr. Harris' office in the Empire Theater Building.

You may know Mr. Wilder as "the professor," or as "the man who wrote *The Bridge of San Luis Rey*," but Mr. Wilder, from now on, wants to be known as Mr. Wilder, the dramatist. . . .

The author of—in addition to *The Bridge—The Woman of Andros* and *Heaven's My Destination* is not exactly making his theatrical debut. Some years ago the town saw his translation of M. André Obey's *Le Viol de Lucrèce*; he has written a quartet of one-acts and an adaption of Ibsen's *A Doll's House,* abetted by the incomparable Ruth Gordon as Nora, is even now hovering in Chicago preparatory to a descent upon Manhattan. Nevertheless:

"I feel," says Mr. Wilder, "that my whole life has been an apprenticeship to writing for the theater.

"You see (eagerly) imaginative story telling consists of telling a number of lies in order to convey a truth; it is a rearrangement of falsehoods which, if it is done honestly, results in verity.

"Now, the thing which most appeals to me about the theater is the absence of editorial comment. There is arrangement, of course, but at least you do not have in the theater, as in the novel, a single fallible human being claiming Godlike omniscience.

"To be sure, it is something of an illusion, but I regard it as a great good."

Mr. Wilder leaned back in his chair, lit another cigarette and went on. One felt as though one were in an especially pleasant classroom.

"Another thing. It is always now on the stage. The stage lives in the pure present; it offers always the pure action and not someone's digestion of that action. . . .

"The play—well, you might say that it is kind of an attempt at complete immersion into everything about a New Hampshire village which, I hope, is gradually felt by the audience to be an allegorical representation of all life.

"It is an idea which has teased me for a long while, but you could say that it was really done— most of it—last summer in a little hotel near Zurich.

"You know, I'm a Wisconsin boy from State of Maine stock, but I spent six summers tutoring in a New Hampshire camp and six summers as a guest of the MacDowell Colony at Peterborough and you can't help but be absorbed by the New Hampshire quality.

"How would I define that? Why, it's independence, understatement—a dry, humorous sense, and, within the walls of the home, a wonderful, congenial homeliness. Lacking in warmth? Not if you know the idiom.

"I used to think about them on the evening walks of twelve summers. There are others I know better, but this is basically a generalization, and it is hard to generalize about one's neighbors.

"I wanted to pile up a million details of daily living, with some sense of the whole in living and dying—San Luis Rey, if you please. I think it the business of writing to restore that sense of the whole."

February 13, 1938—Nine Days after Opening

"A Village Against the Life of the Stars": *Our Town*'s First Preface

No doubt at the request of Brooks Atkinson, Wilder published what he boldly titled "A Preface for *Our Town*" in the *New York Times* on February 13, 1938. The play was safely lodged in the Morosco Theatre when it appeared on page one of the paper's Sunday Arts section. Throughout his life Wilder referred to his formative experience in Rome (1920–21) while studying archaeology. This influence is more than suggested in the excerpt from a letter Wilder wrote to his family in 1921, which concludes this Reading.

For a while in Rome I lived among archeologists, and ever since I find myself occasionally looking at the things about me as an archeologist will look at them a thousand years hence. Rockefeller Center will be reconstructed in imagination from the ruins of its foundations. How high was it? A thesis will be written on the bronze plates found in New York's detritus heaps—"Tradesmen's Entrance," "Night Bell."

In Rome I was led through a study of the plumbing on the Palatine Hill. A friend of mine could ascribe a date, "within ten years," to every fragment of cement made in the Roman Republic and early Empire.

An archeologist's eyes combine the view of the telescope with the view of the microscope. He reconstructs the very distant with the help of the very small.

It was something of this method that I brought

to a New Hampshire village. I spent parts of six summers tutoring at Lake Sunapee and six at the MacDowell Colony at Peterborough. I took long walks through scores of upland villages.

And the archeologist's and the social historian's points of view began to mingle with another unremitting preoccupation which is the central theme of the play: What is the relation between the countless "unimportant" details of our daily life, on the one hand, and the great perspectives of time, social history, and current religious ideas, on the other?

What is trivial and what is significant about any one person's making a breakfast, engaging in a domestic quarrel, in a "love scene," in dying? To record one's feelings about this question is necessarily to exhibit the realistic detail of life, and one is at once up against the problem of realism in literature. . . .

I wished to record a village's life on the stage, with realism and with generality.

The stage has a deceptive advantage over the novel—in that lighted room at the end of the darkened auditorium things seem to be half caught up into generality already. The stage cries aloud its mission to represent the Act in Eternity. So powerful is the focus that it brings to bear on any presented occasion that every lapse of the author from his collaborative intensity is doubly conspicuous: the truth tumbles down into a heap of abject truths and the result is doubly trivial.

So I tried to restore significance to the small details of life by removing scenery. The spectator through lending his imagination to the action restages it inside his own head.

In its healthiest ages the theater has always exhibited the least scenery. Aristophanes' *The Clouds*—423 B.C. Two houses are represented on the stage; inside of one of them we see two beds. Strepsiades is talking in his sleep about his racehorses. A few minutes later he crosses the stage to Socrates' house, the Idea Factory, the "Thinkery." In the Spanish theater Lope de Vega put a rug in the middle of the scene—it was a raft in mid-ocean bearing a castaway. The Elizabethans, the Chinese used similar devices.

The theater longs to represent the symbols of things, not the things themselves. All the lies it tells—the lie that that young lady is Caesar's wife; the lie that people can go through life talking in blank verse; the lie that that man just killed that man—all those lies enhance the one truth that is there—the truth that dictated the story, the myth. The theater asks for as many conventions as possible. A convention is an agreed-upon falsehood, an accepted untruth. When the theater pretends to give the real thing in canvas and wood and metal it loses something of the realer thing which is its true business. Ibsen and Chekhov carried realism as far as it could go, and it took all their genius to do it. Now the camera is carrying it on and is in great "theoretical peril" of falling short of literature. (In a world of actual peril that "theoretical peril" looks very farfetched, but ex–college professors must be indulged.)

But the writing of the play was not accompanied by any such conscious argumentation as this. It sprang from a deep admiration for those little white towns in the hills and from a deep devotion to the

theater. These are but the belated gropings to recon-
struct what may have taken place when the play first
presented itself—the life of a village against the life of
the stars.

In an earlier draft of the play there were some
other lines that led up to those which now serve as
its motto. The Stage Manager has been talking about
the material that is being placed in the cornerstone of
the new bank at Grover's Corners, material that has
been chemically treated so that it will last a thousand
or two thousand years. He suggests that this play has
been placed there so that future ages will know more
about the life of the average person; more than just
the Treaty of Versailles and the Lindbergh Flight—
see what I mean?

Well, people a thousand years from now, in the
provinces North of New York at the beginning of the
Twentieth Century, people ate three times a day—
soon after dawn, at noon, and at sunset.

Every seventh day, by law and by religion, there
was a day of rest and all work came to a stop.

The religion at that time was Christianity, but
I guess you have other records about Christianity.

The domestic set-up was marriage, a binding
relation between a male and one female that lasted
for life.

. . . Anything else? Oh, yes, when people died
they were buried in the ground just as they were.

Well, people a thousand years from now, this is
the way we were—in our growing-up, in our marrying, in our doctoring, in our living, and in our dying.

Now let's get back to our day in Grover's
Corners. . . .

Thornton Wilder to his family, from Rome, 1921:

> I went with an archeological party the other day to
> a newly discovered tomb of about the first century;
> it was under a street near the center of the city, and
> while by candle-light we peered at faded paintings of
> a family called Aurelius, symbolic representations of
> their dear children and parents borne graciously away
> by winged spirits playing in gardens and adjusting
> their Roman robes, the street-cars of today rushed
> over the loves and pieties and habits of the Aurelius
> family, while the same elements were passing over
> in Orelio families that will be as great an effort to
> recover two thousand years from now, as pleasing an
> effort, and as humanizing.

"Take Your Pencil . . ."

On May 2, 1938, *Our Town* received the Pulitzer Prize for
drama. The press came calling. To the clearly bewitched
reporter from *The Sun* (New York), Henry Strickler, Wilder
granted a classic, wide-ranging interview published on
May 14. He was particularly interested in talking about
the charge that his play was guilty of the crime of
sentimentality—and speak he did as we see in this excerpt
from Strickler's piece:

> Thornton Wilder and the reporter were sitting at
> a desk in the Jed Harris office, trying to launch an
> interview. Plainly the situation was out of hand.
>   Mr. Wilder had answered the preliminary ques-
> tions as to where he had been, how long he was going

to be in New York and how it feels to be the author of a Pulitzer Prize winning novel, *The Bridge of San Luis Rey,* 1928, and a Pulitzer Prize winning play, *Our Town,* 1938.

The reporter, searching the folds of his ignorance for an opening, asked Mr. Wilder where he got his story ideas. Mr. Wilder said they came to him on hikes and in the shower and places. The reporter couldn't remember having broken out with anything but a sweat, sunburn and a rash on hikes. Nor could he recall ever having got anything out of a shower but water, a lingering case of athlete's foot and a nasty bruise. So he just stared at Mr. Wilder, who can walk a mile, take a shower and come down with a full-grown second act.

Mr. Wilder broke the uncomfortable silence by guessing correctly that the reporter was from the Mid-West, a fact constantly betrayed by a rustic inflection of speech. The interview threatened to fall off into football amid many inane pleasantries, but Mr. Wilder, sensing an impasse, took the bull by the horns.

"Take your pencil," he ordered, getting out of his chair. He flicked the ash from his cigarette, made two complete hikes around the room in meditation and then began dictating in short, easily penciled phrases.

"Many people have charged the play *Our Town* of being sentimental. The charge seems to be that the home life of the people represented in the play is too uniformly felicitous and the description of the state after death too literal and too idyllic. It is true that village life anywhere presents a proportional element of boredom, small-minded community interference and tragic occasions.

"The literary description of New England has generally occupied itself with similar disproportionate descriptions of avarice and horrifying behavior of the remote farmers whose families' consanguinity, isolation and back-breaking work have developed occasions of violence and crime."

Mr. Wilder was by this time circling the room at the rate of about two revolutions per paragraph.

"The proportion of good and ill in *Our Town*," he continued, "has been frankly cast on the happier side because it is established as a view of the village of 1901 seen through the eyes of 1938.

"Eight out of ten find that memory has selected from their earlier years the more touching and affectionate aspects of their early life. Death, separation and distance have condoned whatever elements are painful."

"Isn't that true?" Mr. Wilder asked, directly addressing the reporter.

"Absolutely," the reporter replied. "What was that last word?"

"Painful," Mr. Wilder said, and started circling again.

"As to the description of the afterlife," he continued, "nothing is more surprising to me than being told that it is original, for it is a transcript of the tone of the first of ten cantos of Dante's "Purgatory" where the newly dead are shown in patient waiting, being—quote—weaned away—unquote—from the attachments of their earthly life and in expectation of some ultimate purification and translation, a doctrine held as an article of faith for many centuries.

"Sentimentality may be described as the distortion of the objective facts of experience felt by the majority of mature persons, a distortion upon material to satisfy wishful fancies that spring from personal identification with the characters in situations presented."

Mr. Wilder sank into his chair in silence in the nick of time. The reporter was about to suffer a stroke of writer's cramp. Mr. Wilder reached over into a bowl of hitherto unnoticed candy and began popping pieces into his mouth while he meditated.

7. Wilder vs. Harris:
Before and After

The inside flap of the dust jacket of the first reading edition of *Our Town* listed seven gorgeous raves hailing not "Thornton Wilder's new play," but "the Jed Harris production of *Our Town*." This is understandable. In 1938 Thornton Wilder was a new face on Broadway and Jed Harris was a theatrical legend eager to regain his footing and fame. The next two sections open the door on the subject of their stormy collaboration and how it played out in their differing views about the tone of the play.

"Lean, dark, and hungry looking," "scorched with ambition," marked by "a remarkable set of phobias" and "hatreds"—these are a few of the adjectives Richard Maney employs in his portrait of the producer-director Jed Harris in *Fanfare* (1957). Maney concludes with these words about the Broadway legend who appeared on the cover of *Time* on September 3, 1928: "Whatever demons have pursued him, he has a knowledge of the theater and a skill in it unmatched by any of his fellows. There are no peaks he might not have scaled had he cared to muffle his malice. The obstacles which stymied him were his own creations." Martin Gottfried subtitled his 1984 biography of Harris "The Curse of Genius." He concludes his recital of Harris's brilliance and self-destructive behavior: "[Harris] had predicted before it began that he'd burn out young. Instead, arrogance, egotism, cruelty, and Machiavellianism had kept his talent from being spent and that was his greatest tragedy."

Harris was the price Wilder paid for the success of his *Our Town*. He paid it with gritted teeth, moments of great anger (unusual with Wilder), and admiration. He did so because he also saw what Maney saw in Harris, "a knowledge of the theater and a skill in it unmatched by any of his fellows." This was the Harris that Wilder admired so much when they became close friends in the late twenties; and this was the Harris that his Yale classmates could still recall vividly twenty years later when they wrote of the undergraduate who once "lived in Welch [Hall] and read Ibsen for breakfast." (Wilder may have known Harris during the latter's abbreviated stay as a Yale student.)

Like a moth drawn to a flame, Wilder made the relationship with Harris in 1937–38 needlessly stressful. First, because he knew it would "hurt Jed's feelings," he elected not to mount *Our Town* through his own highly regarded agent, Harold Freedman. Second, he did not invoke the powers he had under the production contract—signed ten days before the Princeton performance—that forbade changes in the script without his approval. He rectified the first mistake immediately after the play opened, a decision that infuriated Harris. (Freedman's first job was to deal with bounced checks from Harris's office.) The second Wilder fixed over time by virtue of the fact that, at the end of the theatrical day, he controlled the printed page. Where *Our Town* is concerned, this process partially ended in 1957 when Harper and Row published the playwright's "final" approved version—the one used in this edition—and only completely ended in 2013, with release of the play's corrected acting edition published by Samuel French.

What follows lifts the curtain on Wilder's differences with Harris regarding additions and deletions in his manuscript. All stemmed from one root complaint: Wilder's view that Harris was turning his play into a folksy drama for two acts connected to a harrowing last act that left the audience in too many tears.

Before: Wilder's Critical Response to Harris's Directing Choices

*Written and sealed
Noon Jan 22 - 1938*

4 WEST 43ᴿᴰ STREET
NEW YORK

*The following Elements in the
Production of "Our Town" are
likely to harm and perhaps
shipwreck its effectiveness*

The first page of Wilder's handwritten, sealed note regarding Jed Harris's direction of *Our Town*

On the afternoon of the Princeton opening, Wilder wrote and sealed this note in which he outlines his grievances regarding Jed Harris's direction of *Our Town*. Isabel Wilder, his sister, opened it at the time of the play's first New York revival in 1944, and again before the play's 1946 production in London. Both productions were directed by Harris (with Isabel as the playwright's representative), and concluded his contractual rights in the play. There is no evidence that Harris ever read this note—or wanted to. It is printed in its entirety here.

The following Elements in the Production of "*Our Town*" are likely to harm and perhaps shipwreck its effectiveness:

1. The First Act—and in large measure the play—is in danger of falling into trivial episodes, through

business"—but "Twins, eh? I declare, this town's getting bigger every year."

Page 15. Mrs. Webb, after saying ". . . That's how I got to see the Atlantic Ocean, y'know," does not give the speech about "biggest fools coming from Boston." The scene is concluded by Mrs. Gibbs saying: "Oh, I'm sorry I mentioned it. Only it seems to me that once in your life before you die, you ought to see a country where they don't talk in English and don't think in English, and don't even want to."

Page 25. The Stage Manager at the conclusion of the speech is requested to retain both the words and the spirit of the words: "So—people a thousand years from now—this is the way we were, etc."

Page 50. After the words ". . . and particularly the days when you were first in love;" I wish the speech to continue (as in all published texts): "when you were like a person sleeping [sic] walking, and you didn't quite see the street you were walking in, and you didn't quite hear everything that was said to you."

If the actor feels unable to cope with them he may omit the next two sentences in the French Edition.

Page 58. By inadvertence or a typist's error the following phrase was omitted from the "French" edition, though it is in the "library" edition and was used by Frank Craven. After: ". . . interested in quantity; but I think she's interested in quality, too—" comes:" —that's why I'm in the ministry."

The author particularly requests those responsible for maintaining the continued freshness of performances to watch the following passages which experience has shown are likely to become conventional with repetition:

Act III. The speeches of the seated dead must be kept "matter of fact" and un-lugubrious.

Act II. Emily is to refrain from tears and sobbing after she has entered the Drugstore.

Act II. George with his mother and Emily with her father in the scene immediately prior to the wedding are to use moderation in weeping and embracing.

Act II. Mrs. Webb in her address to the audience prior to the wedding is to use restraint in emphasis and not to weep or sob at all.

—Thornton Wilder

Special Features and Legacy

—〰—

8. Wilder as Actor

The Berkshire Theatre Festival production of *Our Town*, August 1939: Thornton Wilder (the Stage Manager) with Ann Mason (Mrs. Gibbs) and Ethel Fund (Mrs. Webb)

During the Broadway run, Wilder filled in for two weeks as the Stage Manager for Frank Craven in September 1938. Taking account of his royalty income, he charged a reduced fee of a hundred dollars a week, which he donated to the Actors Fund. Acting made him a better playwright, he often said. It also allowed him, that September, to delete lines that Harris had inserted into his play.

Wilder appeared in the role of the Stage Manager in five summer stock productions of *Our Town* in 1939–40. After the war he acted in both *Our Town* and *The Skin of Our Teeth*. In total, he performed the role of the Stage Manager some twelve times in summer stock—his last appearance at Williamstown in 1959 when he was sixty-two.

How did he play the role? Avoiding Craven's "soft Irish whimsy," he always "tried to play it straight," as he informed a *New York Times* reporter covering his final appearance in the role in 1959.

The College of Wooster production of *Our Town*, May 1950, with Thornton Wilder as the Minister in Act II

In May 1950, a local reporter saw it this way when Wilder appeared as the Stage Manager at the College of Wooster in Ohio (pictured above).

Mr. Wilder plays the stage manager with a casual informality that is somewhat deceptive. He is confidential, humorous, intense, philosophical by turns, but always so informal that you do not for some time appreciate the rhythmical control with which he shapes the play. The immense air of reality which infuses the play results from his apparently simple but intense demonstration of its fundamental themes. I forgot at times that he was acting; then I was not sure whether he was practicing the art that conceals art or demonstrates the fundamental truths of the play so impressively and effectively because he so intensely believed them. Whatever the art, I found myself eagerly awaiting his every reappearance because he established for me a more intimate connection with the stage than I have often felt.—F.W.M. (*Wooster Daily Record,* May 10, 1950)

9. Wilder as Adviser

Wilder advises (left to right) Bertrand Mitchell (director), Jennifer Holt (Emily), and John Stearns (George)

Although playing the role as naturally as possible, Wilder also saw the Stage Manager's character evolve from a friendly to a distant presence as the play progressed. In a letter of May 31, 1975, written seven months before his death, Wilder wrote to Michael Kahn this advice about how to perform the part of the Stage Manager. At the time, Kahn was preparing to direct *Our Town* at the American Shakespeare Theatre with Fred Gwynne cast in the role:

He now grows from a small-town cracker-barrel, ruminative philosopher—always with a slight smile coming and going—to an almost supernatural spirit presiding over the town affairs. In the last act, he stands gazing over the heads of the audience with a slight smile when Emily asks: "But it's time isn't it?—I can . . . ?" His smile is still relaxed; he nods but he doesn't face her.

Wilder served as an informal adviser when the Peterborough Players first performed *Our Town* in 1940. They have since performed it six more times; the last production, in 2008, starred the late James Whitmore.

What did he advise? The *Manchester Union-Leader* reported him saying that he "never meant that cemetery scene to be so depressing," a view that led the director, who stood firm for a belief in eternal life, to plan to have the dead do "natural things like shelling peas or knitting and smoking." Whether Wilder approved of such an approach is not known. (He almost certainly did not.) What is known is that he advised the cast of Elizabeth Dillon's production at the Trenton Central High School in Trenton, New Jersey, in 1948, to handle act 3 with restraint (no doubt he had Jed Harris's *Our Town* in mind):

There is one injunction I always like to recommend: The last act is not to be played lugubriously. The seated dead are tranquil and the remarks about the weather are spoken in a perfectly matter-or-fact voice. The Stage Manager's remarks are kept "dry" also,— important things but assured and neither with emotion nor edification,—i.e., statements. Some companies, to my distress have not only staged the last act in darkness but with long doleful pauses,—and have "telegraphed" that gloom throughout the preceding acts! The whole play is set in the daily, daily life that we know and which particularly in New England is understated.

10. Wilder Abroad

Isabel Wilder (1900–95), a novelist and graduate of the Yale School of Drama, served as Thornton's deputy for many years. These excerpts from a letter to their older brother, Amos, written January 24, 1946, paint a lively picture of interest in *Our Town* and *The Skin of Our Teeth* in pre- and postwar Europe and Japan, and describe the foundation of Wilder's highly visible role in European, especially German, artistic and academic circles for many years. In 1973, Arena Stage (Washington, DC) took *Our Town* to the Soviet Union. The production was an enormous success.

Wilder was a great admirer of the fearless Elsa Merlini. "Shades of Dante" refers to the influence of Dante's *Purgatorio*, which Wilder taught at the University of Chicago, on setting the tone in Act III. Merlini is pictured on the opposite page with two unidentified actors in a production of *Piccola Città* in Milan in 1946.

Elsa Merlini (Emily) in *Piccola Città*, Milan, 1946

News from Abroad: Letter to Amos

Dear Amos and Family,

Let's see now, OUR TOWN. War stopped the plans for the English production slated for early 1940. This is interesting,—It was done by Red Cross (U.S.) and U.S.O. with a couple of English actors added in London for Armed Services only. It created such excitement and success that the "great" of the English theatre heard about it sent letters to the London Times (DAME Sybil Thorndike, Charles Cochrane, etc.) asking that in the "interest of Anglo-American" culture and relations and understanding, etc. it be given to the whole English public. Army orders forbade that. But the British government's attention was brought to the matter and in the autumn of 1944 they were to do the extraordinary thing of issuing permits for a company of professionals to go from New York with a production to tour England and settle down in London. (I was going.) The Battle of the Bulge stopped that, now it is to be, main characters American, directed by Jed Harris, original director-producer, produced there by Hugh Beaumont (foremost English firm), minor casts English, by April first.

In 1939 it was done in Rome by Elsa Merlini, leading Italian actress who has her own company. The opening night a leading Fascist politico tried to stop the performance, he and his group in the audience started catcalls and speeches. Merlini came to the front of the stage and above the uproar asked the audience if they wanted her to go on. They cried yes, yes, and the rebels were thrown out. Their complaint had been that it was an anti-Fascist play. Good plays, better plays were written by Italians but weren't produced while undeserving foreign importations were done instead.

Merlini has toured Italy for years; with it in her repertory "Piccola Citta" is a household word. Thornton was told by her, (he met her several times in Rome and Naples last winter) and others (he did not see the production) that many Italians did not completely understand Act I and II but they adored and understood Act III and waited patiently for Act III. Shades of Dante!

It was done long ago in Zurich and was a great success; ditto Skin [The Skin of Our Teeth]. Sweden. Buenos Aires. Pirated and performed in Spain. It was the first foreign play to be done in Berlin shortly after the Occupation. The Russian authorities stopped it in 3 days. Rumors give the reason it was "unsuitable for the Germans so soon,—too democratic." It is now in preparation in the American Section. We have heard direct, aired program and reviews from Munich. Wonderfully played there. A great and moving success. A letter from our Swiss agent who handles the German translation says it is being done everywhere in Germany—they somehow get the script and do it. Yugo-slavia asked T. for it when he was there,—in the interest of cultural relations. Budapest, Czechoslovakia. The requests come in every day. A Rockefeller Doctor travelling in Holland said he'd seen a U.S.O. performance. Our boys adored it. (As everywhere. It was out 8 months for our homesick troops.) Native Hollanders heard about it, asked for it, and have done it themselves. Today I am answering a letter from the University of Delft. The University is having a festival to celebrate Holland's liberation. They want to do SKIN OF OUR TEETH, saying it speaks for them, the whole world at this time rising out of ruins. Our authorities in Japan have written for permission to have Our Town translated and given to the Japanese native theatres for its importance of the American and democratic way of life and the art and literature it represents. Etc. Etc. It was done in prison of war camps. . . . Does this answer your question? You can't say too much!

Love to all,

[Isabel]

Masahiko Yakou

Act III of *Our Town*, 2011 production at the New National Theatre, Tokyo, Japan. With Kazuki Kosakai (Stage Manager) and Yuki Saito (Mrs. Gibbs), directed by Hachiya Mizutani.

Our Town continues to be played around the world, with productions in more than thirty countries since 2000.

L'Envoi

—m—

11. Final Thoughts: "Value above All Price . . ."

OUR TOWN Quoted from T.W.:

The play "" is an attempt to find a value above all
price for the smallest events in our daily
life.

But that is absurd. The generations of men follow upon
one another in apparently endless repetition. They
are born; they grow up; they marry; they have children;
they die. Where shall we seek a "value above all
price" in these recurrent situations?

Wilder's gloss in his handwriting on his famous lines.

No line is more quoted in theater programs about *Our Town*
than this sentence from Wilder's 1957 preface to *Three Plays*.
Among his papers is his handwritten editorial note, probably
written in the 1960s, in which he calls this line "absurd." The
note is quoted in full below. Did he make this annotation for
a reason—perhaps simply for the record? We don't know. But
it is probably Thornton Wilder's last word on what he felt he
had accomplished when he wrote a play called *Our Town*.

The play is an attempt to find a value above all price
for the smallest events in our daily life. But that is
absurd. The generations of men follow upon one

another in apparently endless repetition. They are born; they grow up; they marry; they have children; they die. Where shall we seek a "value above all price" in these recurrent situations?

The audience in a theatre watches human beings caught up in the happy or unhappy vicissitudes of circumstance. The audience knows more about what most concerns the characters than they can ever know themselves. The audience is given a more than human vision.

In the last act of "*Our Town*" the author places upon the stage a character who—like the member of the audience—partakes of the "smallest events of our daily life" and is also a spectator of them.

She learns that each life—though it appears to be a repetition among millions—can be felt to be inestimably precious. Though the realization of it is present to us seldom, briefly, and incommunicably. At that moment there are no walls, no chairs, no tables: all is inward. Our true life is in the imagination and in the memory.

Acknowledgments

~~~

The Overview of this volume is constructed in large part from Thornton Wilder's words in unpublished letters, journals, business records, and publications not easy to come by.

Many Wilder fans have helped me with this volume. Space permits me to extend thanks to only a few—Barbara Whitepine, Catharine Wilder Guiles, Gilbert Kerlin, Glen Swanson, Camille Dee, David R. Woods, Noa Wheeler; Robert Freedman and Selma Luttinger of the Robert A. Freedman Dramatic Agency; and Barbara Hogenson and Nicole Verity of the Barbara Hogenson Agency. Thomas Clements III kindly provided details about Wilder's stabs at longitude and latitude. Dr. Patricia Willis and the able staff of the Beinecke Library always deserve special applause, as does Penelope Niven, whose assistance has been invaluable. From start to finish, it has been inspiring to work with Donald Margulies.

If there are errors in the Overview, I take responsibility for them and welcome corrections.

Addendum Acknowledgments

I thank Barbara Hogenson and Rosey Strub and Harper-Collins editor Jennifer Civiletto for their invaluable help with this edition. With admiration and affection, I wish also to recall the names of Penelope Niven and J. D. McClatchy, two gifted Wilder fans sadly no longer with us, who helped us all do our best.

Unpublished Material

Unless otherwise identified in the Overview and Readings, or noted here, all unpublished materials are taken from one of two sources: the holdings in the Thornton Wilder Papers in the Yale Collection of American Literature at the Beinecke Rare Book and Manuscript Library, or the Wilder family's own holdings, including many of Thornton Wilder's legal and agency papers. Silent corrections in spelling and punctuation have been made when deemed appropriate. Wilder's correspondence with Alexander Woollcott is held at Harvard in the Houghton Library's Harvard Theatre Collection, and his letters to Lady Sibyl Colefax are housed in Special Collections, Fales Library, New York University. The original production of *Our Town*'s "prompt script" is held in the Harvard Theatre Collection, Houghton Library, Harvard University (TS 3494.750), and the Collection's assistance in supplying a reproducible page from it (Reading 3) is acknowledged. Wilder's letter to Sol Lesser (Overview), producer of the *Our Town* film, dated "Easter night [1940]" is held in the Department of Special Collections, University Research Library, University of California, Los Angeles. Fred E. Walker played the part of Dr. Gibbs in Trenton Central High School's 1948 production of *Our Town*. The letter, held by him and quoted from in Reading 9, was sent to the cast through Dean Frederic Adams of Trinity Cathedral, Trenton. The courtesies extended by these institutions and by Mr. Walker are gratefully acknowledged.

Quotations and Publications

Unless credited in the text, in the Afterword, Jeremy McCarter's words are taken from "The Genius of Grover's Corners," his review of *Thornton Wilder: Collected Plays & Writings on Theater*, published in the *New York Times Book Review*, April 1, 2007, p. 27. A. R. Gurney's words are found in his Introduction to *The Collected Short Plays of Thornton Wilder, Volume II* (New York: Theatre Communication Group Press, 1999, p. xvi); Edward Albee's remarks are from an interview given in April 1999 for a projected Thornton Wilder documentary. J. D. McClatchy uses the quoted phrase in talks about editing Wilder's works and serving as librettist for the *Our Town* opera.

Reading 2, from *The Woman of Andros*, is taken from the HarperCollins Perennial edition (New York, 2006), pp. 148–49. Wilder's discussion on the themes in the novel is found on p. 24 of the spring issue of Marshall Field & Company's *Fashions of the Hour*, an influential publication in the period. *Pullman Car Hiawatha*, and the other one-act plays mentioned, are available to general readers in *The Collected Short Plays of Thornton Wilder, Volume I* (New York: Theatre Communications Group Press, 1997) and in individual and collected acting additions (New York: Samuel French, Inc., 2013). Sutherland Denlinger conducted the *New York World-Telegram* interview of December 7, 1937 (Reading 6).

It was reprinted by Jackson R. Bryer, Ed., in *Conversations with Thornton Wilder* (Jackson: University Press of Mississippi, 1992), pp. 15–17. Wilder's "A Preface for *Our Town*," (Reading 6) is reprinted in *American Characteristics and Other Essays* (New York: Harper & Row, 1979; Authors Guild Backprint edition, 2000), pp. 100–3. Thomas Coley's *"Our Town" Remembered,* a pamphlet dedicated to Isabel Wilder (Overview), was published privately in 1982.

All rights for all published and unpublished work by Thornton Wilder are reserved by the Wilder Family LLC.

Photographs

Unless otherwise credited herein, the photographs in this edition are held in the Thornton Wilder Papers in the Yale Collection of American Literature at the Beinecke Rare Book and Manuscript Library, or by the Wilder family, and are used with permission of the Wilder Family LLC.

I am grateful to Sally Higginson Begley for providing the 1939 Berkshire Theatre Festival production photograph shown in Reading 8 (STF Archive), to the staff of the Peterborough Players for the 1940 photograph (Reading 9), and to the MacDowell Colony for the picture of Veltin Studio (Reading 4). Catharine Kerlin Wilder (1906–2005), the bride shown in the first photograph (Reading 1), graciously consented to its use. The two Vandamm photographs of the original Broadway production are reproduced with the permission of the Billy Rose Theatre Collection, New York Public Library for the Performing Arts, Astor, Lenox, and Tilden Foundations.

We thank the management of the Hotel Belvoir in Rüschlikon, Switzerland (Reading 4) for providing a photograph of the hotel as Wilder would have known it in 1937.

The two photographs from the College of Wooster's 1950 production of *Our Town*—the author's photograph on page 197, showing Thornton Wilder playing the Stage Manager in Act I, and the photograph on page 178 of Wilder playing the role of the minister in Act II—appear with the permission of Special Collections, the College of Wooster Libraries, Wooster, Ohio.

Source Material and
Subsidiary Works

—⚬⚬⚬—

(available since 2000)

Sources

Major new resources for the general audience and for teachers and theater professionals who are interested in learning more about Thornton Wilder's life and work have become available since the first edition of this book. For ongoing information visit the Wilder family's website, www.thorntonwilder.com, and the Thornton Wilder Society's website, www.twilder society.org. Recent titles using extensive archival holdings never before available to researchers include: *Thornton Wilder: A Life* by Penelope Niven (HarperCollins, 2012); *The Selected Letters of Thornton Wilder*, edited by Robin G. Wilder and Jackson R. Bryer (HarperCollins, 2008); The Library of America's three-volume edition of Wilder's fiction and drama, edited by J. D. McClatchy (*Collected Plays & Writings on Theater* [2007], *The Bridge of San Luis Rey and Other Novels* 1926–1948 [2009], *The Eighth Day, Theophilus North & Autobiographical Writings* [2011]); HarperCollins/ Harper Perennial individual editions of Wilder's novels and major dramas with Forewords and Afterwords by contemporary authors. For examples of recent scholarship on Wilder see *Thornton Wilder: New Perspectives,* edited by Jackson R. Bryer and Lincoln Konkle (Northwestern University Press, 2013); *Thornton Wilder & Amos Wilder: Writing Religion in Twentieth-Century America,* by Christopher J. Wheatley (University of Notre Dame Press, 2011); and *Thornton Wilder in Collaboration: Collected Essays on His Drama and Fiction,* edited by Jackson R. Bryer, Judith P. Hallett, and Edyta K. Oczkowicz (Cambridge Scholars Publishing, 2018).

It must be underscored that the *Our Town* material in *The Selected Letters* and Penelope Niven's treatment of the play's sources in her groundbreaking biography represent essential new information, and are thus required reading for a fuller understanding of the work.

Subsidiary Works

The *Our Town* opera, composed by Ned Rorem with libretto by J. D. McClatchy and managed by Boosey and Hawkes, had its world premiere at Indiana University on February 25, 2006; *The Return,* a modern dance interpretation from GroundWorks DanceTheater inspired by *Our Town* and developed by David Shimotakahara, premiered on February 4, 2011 in Cleveland, Ohio; *OT: Our Town,* a documentary by Scott Kennedy on the making of *Our Town* in inner-city Dominguez High School in Compton, California, was released by Black Valley Films in 2002.

About the Author

In his quiet way, THORNTON NIVEN WILDER was a revolution-
ary writer who experimented boldly with literary forms and
themes, from the beginning to the end of his long career.
"Every novel is different from the others," he wrote when he

was seventy-five. "The theater (ditto). . . . The thing I'm writing now is again totally unlike anything that preceded it." Wilder's richly diverse settings, characters, and themes are at once specific and global. Deeply immersed in classical as well as contemporary literature, he often fused the traditional and the modern in his novels and plays, all the while exploring the cosmic in the commonplace. In a January 12, 1953, cover story, *Time* took note of Wilder's unique "planetary mind"— his ability to write from a vision that was at once American and universal.

A pivotal figure in the history of twentieth-century letters, Wilder was a novelist and playwright whose works continue to be widely read and produced in this new century. He is the only writer to have won the Pulitzer Prize for both fiction and drama. His second novel, *The Bridge of San Luis Rey*, received the fiction award in 1928, and he won the prize twice in drama, for *Our Town* in 1938 and *The Skin of Our Teeth* in 1943. His other novels are *The Cabala, The Woman of Andros, Heaven's My Destination, The Ides of March, The Eighth Day*, and *Theophilus North*. His other major dramas include *The Matchmaker*, which was adapted as the internationally acclaimed musical comedy *Hello, Dolly!*, and *The Alcestiad*. Among his innovative, frequently performed shorter plays are *The Happy Journey to Trenton and Camden* and *The Long Christmas Dinner* (1931). In the 1950s, he conceived a unique dramatic series, *The Seven Ages of Man* and *The Seven Deadly Sins*, completing four of the plays he envisioned in each group. Three of the plays were first performed in 1962 as *Plays for Bleecker Street*.

Wilder and his work received many honors, highlighted by the three Pulitzer Prizes, the Gold Medal for Fiction from the American Academy of Arts and Letters, the Order of Merit (Peru), the Goethe-Plakette der Stadt (Germany, 1959), the Presidential Medal of Freedom (1963), the National Book Committee's first National Medal for Literature (1965), and the National Book Award for Fiction (1967).

He was born in Madison, Wisconsin, on April 17, 1897, to Amos Parker Wilder and Isabella Niven Wilder. The family later lived in China and in California, where Wilder was graduated from Berkeley High School. After two years at Oberlin College, he went on to Yale, where he received his undergraduate degree in 1920. A valuable part of his education took place during summers spent working hard on farms in California, Kentucky, Vermont, Connecticut, and Massachusetts. His father arranged these rigorous "shirtsleeve" jobs for Wilder and his older brother, Amos, as part of their initiation into the American experience.

Thornton Wilder studied archaeology and Italian as a special student at the Amerian Academy in Rome (1920–21) and earned a master of arts degree in French literature at Princeton in 1926.

In addition to his talents as playwright and novelist, Wilder was an accomplished teacher, essayist, translator, scholar, lecturer, librettist, and screenwriter. In 1942, he teamed with Alfred Hitchcock to write the first draft of the screenplay for the classic thriller *Shadow of a Doubt,* receiving credit as principal writer and a special screen credit for his "contribution to the preparation" of the production. All but fluent in four languages, Wilder translated and adapted plays by such varied authors as Henrik Ibsen, Jean-Paul Sartre, and André Obey. As a scholar, he conducted significant research on James Joyce's *Finnegans Wake* and the plays of Spanish dramatist Lope de Vega.

Wilder's friends included a broad spectrum of figures on both sides of the Atlantic—Hemingway, Fitzgerald, Alexander Woollcott, Gene Tunney, Sigmund Freud, producer Max

Reinhardt, Katharine Cornell, Ruth Gordon, and Garson Kanin. Beginning in the mid-1930s, Wilder was especially close to Gertrude Stein and became one of her most effective interpreters and champions. Many of Wilder's friendships are documented in his prolific correspondence. Wilder believed that great letters constitute a "great branch of literature." In a lecture entitled "On Reading the Great Letter Writers," he wrote that a letter can function as a "literary exercise," the "profile of a personality," and "news of the soul," apt descriptions of thousands of letters he wrote to his own friends and family.

Wilder enjoyed acting and played major roles in several of his own plays in summer theater productions. He also possessed a lifelong love of music; reading musical scores was a hobby, and he wrote librettos for two operas based on his work: *The Long Christmas Dinner,* with composer Paul Hindemith, and *The Alcestiad,* with composer Louise Talma. Both works premiered in Germany.

Teaching was one of Wilder's deepest passions. He began his teaching career in 1921 as an instructor in French at Lawrenceville, a private secondary school in New Jersey. Financial independence after the publication of *The Bridge of San Luis Rey* permitted him to leave the classroom in 1928, but he returned to teaching in the 1930s at the University of Chicago. For six years, on a part-time basis, he taught courses in comparative literature, classics in translation, and composition. In 1950–51, he served as the Charles Eliot Norton Professor of Poetry at Harvard. Wilder's gifts for scholarship and teaching (he treated the classroom as all but a theater) made him a consummate, much sought-after lecturer in his own country and abroad. After World War II, he held special standing, especially in Germany, as an interpreter of his own country's intellectual traditions and their influence on cultural expression.

During World War I, Wilder had served a three-month stint as an enlisted man in the Coast Artillery section of the army, stationed at Fort Adams, Rhode Island. He volunteered for service in World War II, advancing to the rank of lieutenant colonel in Army Air Force Intelligence. For his service in North Africa and Italy, he was awarded the Legion of Merit, the Bronze Star, the Chevalier Legion d'Honneur, and honorary officership in the Military Order of the British Empire (M.B.E.).

From royalties received from *The Bridge of San Luis Rey*, Wilder built a house for his family in 1930 in Hamden, Connecticut, just outside New Haven. But he typically spent as many as two hundred days a year away from Hamden, traveling to and settling in a variety of places that provided the stimulation and solitude he needed for his work. Sometimes his destination was the Arizona desert, the MacDowell Colony in New Hampshire, Martha's Vineyard, Saratoga Springs, Vienna, or Baden-Baden. He wrote aboard ships, and he often chose to stay in "spas in off-season." He needed a certain refuge when he was deeply immersed in writing a novel or play. Wilder explained his habit to a *New Yorker* journalist in 1959: "The walks, the quiet—all the elegance is present, everything is there but the people. That's it! A spa in off-season! I'll make a practice of it."

But Wilder always returned to "the house *The Bridge* built," as it is still known to this day. He died there of a heart attack on December 7, 1975.

WORKS BY THORNTON WILDER

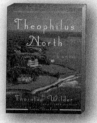

THEOPHILUS NORTH
A Novel

"An extremely entertaining array of American life in a bygone era."
—*New Yorker*

THE BRIDGE OF SAN LUIS REY
A Novel

"One merely has to consider the central question raised by the novel, which, according to Wilder himself, was simply: 'Is there a direction and meaning in the lives beyond the individual's own will?' It is perhaps the largest and most profoundly personal philosophical inquiry that we can undertake. It is the question that defines us as human beings."
—Russell Banks, foreword to *The Bridge of San Luis Rey*

THE CABALA and THE WOMAN OF ANDROS
Two Novels

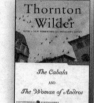

"No matter where and when Wilder's novels take place, his characters grapple with universal questions about the nature of human existence."
—Penelope Niven, author of *Thornton Wilder*

THE EIGHTH DAY
A Novel

"We marvel at a novel of such spiritual ambition."
—John Updike, foreword to *The Eighth Day*

HEAVEN'S MY DESTINATION
A Novel

"If John Steinbeck's mighty *The Grapes of Wrath* is the tragic novel of the Great Depression, then *Heaven's My Destination* is its comic masterpiece."
—J. D. McClatchy, foreword to *Heaven's My Destination*

THE IDES OF MARCH
A Novel

"Full of the wisdom of the ages—as well as satirical observations on man's political instability, loves, joys and terrors."
—*Chicago Tribune*

OUR TOWN
A Play in Three Acts
"Our Town is probably the finest play ever written by an American."
—Edward Albee

THE SELECTED LETTERS OF
THORNTON WILDER
"A remarkable collection. . . . What emerges from these pages is a new and sometimes surprising self-portrait of a great American artist."
—Marian Seldes

THE SKIN OF OUR TEETH
A Play
"For an American dramatist, all roads lead back to Thornton Wilder."
—Paula Vogel, foreword to *The Skin of Our Teeth*

THREE PLAYS
Our Town, The Skin of Our Teeth, and *The Matchmaker*
"These plays are a gift." —John Guare, foreword to *Three Plays*

THE MATCHMAKER
A Farce in Four Acts
"Loud, slap dash and uproarious . . . extraordinarily original and funny."
—*New York Times*

THORNTON WILDER: A LIFE
by Penelope Niven
"The best kind of literary biography, one likely to send the reader back (or perhaps for the first time) to the author's works." —*Washington Post*

failure to build up the two great idea-pillars of the Stage-Manager's interruptions. The Professor's speech has been reduced to pleasant fooling, instead of being made forceful and informative, as I have often requested; the Passage on the future has been watered down, and the actor has not been vigorously directed.

2. The element of the Concrete Localization of the Town has been neglected—in fact, the Director has an astonishingly weak sense of visual reconstruction. Characters talk to one another from Mrs. Webb's back door to Main Street; and from one end of Main Street to another in the same tone of voice they use when they are in the same "room." They stroll practically in and out of Main Street when they are in a house; Emily's grave is one minute here and soon after there.

3. In spite of express promises to remove them a series of interpolations in the First Act remain; each one of these has the character of amiable dribbling, robbing the text of its nervous compression, from which alone can spring the sense of Significance in the Trivial Acts of Life, which is the subject of the play.

4. The recent alterations to the closing words of Mrs. Gibbs and Emily in Act III are soft, and bathetic.

5. There seems every likelihood that a pseudo-artistic inclination to dim lights will further devitalize the Stage-Manager's long speeches; and the last Act. The eternal principle that the ear does not choose to hear, if the eye is not completely satisfied, particularly applies in this play.

After: Wilder's Notes to Harris Regarding Subsequent Productions of *Our Town*

Despite his efforts during the original production to rid the script of Harris's "tasteless alternations," Wilder discovered that several had crept back into the text as Harris prepared to direct the war-delayed London premiere in 1946. Wilder concluded with an appeal to avoid tears and to keep speeches "un-lugubrious," an adjective he also used in his "Some Suggestions for the Director" in the acting edition. The reading is printed in its entirety. All changes are part of the play today.

April 7, 1946

THE TEXT OF *"OUR TOWN"* FOR THE LONDON
AND ALL SUBSEQUENT PRODUCTIONS

In spite of the fact that I left in the Jed Harris offices three copies of the specifically marked Definite Copies of the text of the play, I found during the final rehearsals of the play a number of unauthorized readings were still being used. I called Jed Harris's attention to them; he made notations of the readings, and assured me they would be corrected.

I hereby wish to prepare this memorandum for control of the text as presented in England.

Page references are to the Samuel French Acting Edition.

Page 8. Howie Newsome, the milkman, does not say "Twins, eh? That's good news for a man in my